WATER DANCE

A Lake Michigan Lodge Story

Kathy Fawcett

1

"Merci beaucoup, *Señor*," I said to Luke.

Luke set a warm cup of Swiss chocolate on the desk in our hotel room, then went to lie down on the bed. I heard him plumping the downy pillows to lean against. Without turning to look, I could picture his long, tanned legs stretched out on the luxury linens.

"That's *Monsieur* to you *Madame*, Danke Schön," he said, and I smiled.

We had marveled earlier at how the language changed with every border in Europe.

"Imagine if each state in the U.S. spoke their own language," Luke said.

I couldn't imagine. Although since relocating to my state, Luke insists Michigan residents have their own secret dialect.

"It's not a secret," I had told him, "everybody knows that a *Yooper* is someone from the Upper Peninsula, and a *Fudgie* is a tourist."

"And where, exactly, is *Up North*?" he wanted to know.

"That's easy, it's anywhere north of where you are at any given time," I said, "unless the location is south of Flint—that would just be ridiculous."

"French would be easier," Luke protested.

"You were meant for Michigan," I insisted, with genuine admiration. "You're already showing people where we live on the back of your hand."

It was hard to believe Switzerland was our last country, and this was our last night.

Luke, I knew, wanted the two of us to share the setting sun, and watch it disappear behind the spectacular Matterhorn. We'd be leaving for home in the morning.

After a day of hiking along alpine lakes and wildflowers, I fell into our cool room late this afternoon and let the deep bathtub soak away all the aches in my muscles. Luke called the dining room and asked for our dinner to be sent up.

Now, I was so relaxed I could barely lift a pen to achieve my last task of the day, and of the trip—writing a promised postcard to Aunt June in Florida.

For three glorious July weeks we had been touring northern Spain, France, and now Switzerland by way of Austria. This deferred honeymoon was one magical day after the next, and well worth the eleven month wait.

"Spain was lovely," I said, reading aloud as I wrote. "The Bay of Biscay had islands that looked just like castles."

"Hurry up, you're missing the sunset," Luke said.

"In the Provence region of France," I continued, "the lavender fields were in bloom."

"You know," Luke said, "you'll be back in a few days and can call your aunt."

"I'll do that too," I countered, and continued writing. "Luke and I walked the cobbled streets of Old Town in Saint-Tropez."

"It's just a little card, not a journal," he said.

"True," I said.

I had tried to write a journal of our trip. But it was too much repetition.

Breakfast in France, croissants and marmalade.
Breakfast in Spain, churros and chocolate.
Breakfast in Switzerland, muesli and hard cheese.

Eventually, I decided this particular history need not be recorded—my snug waistband was document enough. I was a walking exhibit, titled: *American Devours Europe.*

That said, I often wished my parents had kept a journal, so I could have some insight and historical reference as I tried to fill their larger-than-life shoes, running their beloved Kerby Lodge on Lake Michigan. But they would have been too busy during the peak seasons, and there was little to write about in the shoulder seasons and frigid winters.

Still, I longed to see their handwriting, and hear about their guests.

I was a hypocrite, of course. But I was determined to stay in the moment with Luke, as I've spent too many years living in the past. Mourning my losses.

Gazing out the window at the tiny Swiss village of Zermatt, I saw lights coming on. They twinkled throughout the town and even dotted the hillside as climbers were tucking in for the night, after a day of bravely ascending the mighty Matterhorn. In the village, a small cemetery held the graves of those who had fallen—dating back to the mid-1800s.

Luke and I were but small specks in the timeline of the world, yet here we were. Looking out at the highest mountains in Europe; church spires rising between us and the hills.

"Here, let me help you with that," Luke said, coming over to where I sat at the desk. He kissed my neck, and then the side of my face—which was warmed by the desk lamp. When he turned the little light off, the setting sun cast us both in a golden glow.

"Having a wonderful time. Wish you were here," he said, softly into my ear.

"You wish Aunt June was here?" I turned to tease Luke, who was no longer looking at the Matterhorn, but at me. As if I were infinitely more mesmerizing than the cathedral-like glacier, frosted with snow and now deep in shadows.

"No," Luke said, gently setting the pen down and taking my hand, which he then used to pull me towards the deep bank of pillows.

"I wish *you* were *here*."

A day later, sleeping against the cold airplane window, I missed those thick downy pillows. Like a puppet on a string, my head now lolled over onto an anemic travel ring propped around my neck. It could barely support my head and cascade of unruly red waves. But at least it absorbed the thin stream of drool traveling from my open mouth.

I'd pop this pillow in the nearest bin when we landed, I decided.

It had served bravely overseas—during several flights, countless train rides, and one tour of duty on an Alpen bus that piped in the *Sound of Music*, while taking us to the gazebo where Liesl and Rolf danced to *I am Sixteen Going on Seventeen.*

Removing my eye mask, I could see Luke was putting his seat upright, and gathering his headphones and newspaper into his backpack. We were getting ready to land in the U.S., I realized, and forced myself to wake up.

It was late here at home—the middle of the night. As we descended, I opened the window shade and looked at the barren roads and sleepy neighborhoods.

Minutes later, taxiing to a gate, the *ding dinging* of phones could be heard throughout the cabin as they reconnected with the network—my own included. People around me began calling loved ones to say they had arrived. Others opened their phones and sent texts. Still others scrolled through their email, and checked the weather.

In my own backpack, my phone was *dinging* as it loaded three weeks' worth of unread messages. On the first night of our trip, Luke had shoved both our phones to the bottom of our mesh laundry bag. We only just fished them out as we packed to come home.

My college intern, Hollis Fanning, had our itinerary—as did my trusted friend Jennifer, who regularly came to the lodge to manage her repurposed furniture store, located in the former carriage house.

"Call if you need me," I said, and they agreed.

Since I hadn't heard a peep, I assumed all was well at Kerby Lodge. But the dinging texts from Hollis now told a different, alarming story. My gasps cut through the white noise of the idling airplane, and Luke looked over at me as I stared at my phone.

"What is it?" he said, "is everyone okay?"

"I'm not sure," I managed to say.

"Is it the lodge? What's going on?" he asked.

I couldn't speak for a moment. Finally, I looked helplessly over at Luke.

"There was a fire..." I said.

"A fire!" he said in alarm.

"And a flood..." I continued, looking up at his shocked face.

Luke was mute, staring at me with his mouth open.

"And an accident," I said.

He held out his hand for my phone and read the messages himself.

Trembling, I was glad to have a husband by my side who would be strong and comforting, and help me through the tragedies that had befallen my lodge while I was away.

"All that's missing is a plague of locusts," Luke said.

2

Kerby Lodge is an out of the way place,
that goes out of the way to make summer amazing.
-KERBY LODGE GUEST BOOK-

Luke was not convinced there had been three disasters. Or even one.

As we waited for our luggage, he explained that Hollis' texts looked more like shorthand than complete thoughts. "My students do this all the time," he said.

I looked back at the first text: *Grt Rm BRNT dwn*

"What else could this be except a fire that destroyed the great room?" I asked.

"Why don't you call Hollis and ask her?" Luke said.

"It's two in the morning," I said.

"She's a college kid," Luke said, "she's probably still up."

"Not this girl," I said.

Luke walked closer to the baggage carousel, and I followed.

"*Fld A FRM*," I sounded out the next text for Luke. "That's a flood in the A-Frame cabin," I said, "of course."

"Or not," Luke said, shrugging.

"Okay, explain this one then," I showed him my phone.

5 HURT in fall

"Yeah, that one looks bad," Luke agreed.

Both our suitcases came towards us, just then, and we grabbed them.

"Look Kaker," he said, using my family nickname, "if there was a fire, a flood, and an accident, I'd be hearing about it. Instead, there's a text from my brother reminding me to send Mom a birthday card. And one from Patrick about season football tickets."

"Nothing," he continued, "about the earth opening up and swallowing Kerby Lodge." He threw his backpack over his shoulder and took my hand for the short walk to long-term parking.

Luke had a point, and my other messages supported it.

Jennifer welcomed us home with no mention of the *Hollis-pocalypse*.

Aunt June said to rest up, and call in a few days.

My friend Chip, who owned a landscape business, left a message returning my call. Yes, he could remove a grove of pines trees from my property. He had a busy schedule, but would squeeze the job in at the end of August. "Stay on me," he said.

There was a text from Stace Wildberry. She was an interior decorator who partnered with her twin brother Jack. Hers was a full, cohesive sentence, but not a happy message. Certainly not one I was eager to share with my weary husband.

"Well, if the lodge *did* burn to cinders, and the A-Frame washed into the Great Lake, it's a good thing we live in your grandmother's old house on the hill," Luke said as we got in the Jeep. "You and I will be in our own bed before you know it."

"About that…" I said.

And as we drove home through the inky summer night, carefully watching for deer and other wildlife along the road, I broke the news to Luke about the one catastrophe I was sure of.

"Stace left me a text," I told him, "it says *House is Not Habitable.*"

"Not habitable," repeated Luke, "we left it very habitable, what happened?"

I told him that workers found water damage—which triggered insurance claims and additional expenses. Walls had to come down, and rotted boards were replaced. A new furnace and water heater were being installed. Plus, the entire house was being checked for mold.

The fact that the leak escaped us didn't surprise me. The house hadn't been lived in year-round since Gram passed away. That is, until Luke and I moved in.

"Tragic," Luke said, his stunned expression visible by the dashboard lights.

This man who had been so flippant about my lodge burning down, was devastated that he couldn't have his own pillow tonight.

"What could possibly go wrong?" I asked Luke a month ago, before we left for Europe.

My own words came back to haunt me now.

The house up the hill, the only actual house on the 12-acre property, had just started to feel like our home. It wasn't a too-small cabin. And it wasn't the big rambling lodge that I'd grown up in. In the words of Goldilocks, the house was *just right*.

And *just right* was what we longed for after our exhausting trip. Like all travelers, we were ready for our own beds and our own bowls of porridge.

We'd even gotten used to Gram's furniture—though most of it was weird and retro, in shades of orange and avocado green. But the shag carpets and 70s wallpaper had to go. What better way than to rip off the bandage, and have everything done while we were away?

Working closely with Jack and Stace, I planned a painless renovation, to be done without any inconvenience to Luke. But as my Scottish Mum Raya used to paraphrase from her favorite poet, *"The best laid schemes o' mice an' men oft go awry, lass."*

Oh brother, did my plan go awry.

Additional messages told us more. Before I knew it, we were turning onto the Kerby Lodge road, where we'd see for ourselves how *Not Habitable* the house really was. We'd also see which of Hollis' texts pointed to actual disasters—and which were the creative shortcuts of a millennial intern.

First, we drove past Gram's dark house, where construction tape blocked off the driveway. Slowing to a near stop, we could spot lumber on top of saw horses, and tarps protecting even more lumber and power tools from the elements.

Not habitable indeed. I could only imagine the chaos inside.

Continuing down the road, the cabins were quiet. But many appeared to be occupied, I noted, which was a pleasant surprise.

As we turned into the circle driveway of the main lodge, the headlights bounced through the pine trees—the ones I wanted Chip to remove—and off of the A-Frame. Which happily, appeared intact. Finally, through the leaded transom window next to the door, I spotted the little lamp I always left on in the great room—the room that had not burned down.

"Och what a relief that Raya's lodge is okay," I said to Luke, exhaling fully for the first time since landing. I heard the emotion and brogue in my voice—the two often going hand in hand. There was *nae* denying it, I was the keeper of Raya Kerby's lodge, life and dreams. Allowing harm to come to any of it was more than I could bear.

I could see Luke smile as he pulled our suitcases out of the Jeep. "Come along, *wee lass*," he said, "let's call it a night."

Before following him into the lodge apartment, I took a moment to stand outside and breathe in the fresh balsam-scented air, and stare up at the starry night sky. A slight breeze off the lake rustled the oak leaves and the pine boughs overhead. An owl hooted softly from the woods. And the moon shone on the rocks and sand on the shore.

"Welcome home," I said quietly to myself, and blew a kiss towards Lake Michigan.

No big reveal for us tonight, I thought with a hint of sadness. Instead, we'd drop our luggage, and our exhausted selves, in my childhood bedroom of the innkeeper's apartment. Luke and I were quiet as we made our way, mindful of guests sleeping in rooms on the other side of the lodge.

I hadn't slept in the apartment in a full year, since before we were married.

"What has happened here?" I exclaimed after bumping into a stack of boxes while reaching for a small lamp. "All these boxes—it feels like a warehouse."

In addition to my own stored items and emergency supplies for winter, a quick search revealed that all three bedrooms were overcrowded with hastily packed boxes from Gram's house, and mysteriously, several boxes marked with my brother-in-law's name.

Daniel Mayne, marketing professional and Luke's brother, came and went in between his gigs. But his stuff should all be in the A-Frame cottage where he usually stays.

"Luke, why is the apartment filled with Daniel's things?" I asked, but Luke was already fast asleep on a pillowcase of yellow daisies, under a summer coverlet of peonies. His jeans and shirt were thrown over one box. His shoes and socks sat on another.

After washing my face, I opened a window to allow the lake breezes to push out the musty air. Then I tossed my own travel clothes next to Luke's, and slipped under the coverlet. Like the boxes, my questions for Hollis were stacking up.

Boxes upon boxes.

Head spinning and mind reeling, I drifted off to sleep pondering brown boxes, and a ribbon of a distant memory—a poem from my college days about boxes and, oddly enough, learning the English language.

> *We'll begin with a box, and the plural is boxes.*
> *But the plural of ox becomes oxen, not oxes.*
> *You may find a mouse, or nest full of mice.*
> *Yet the plural of house is houses, not hice...*

3

I stared at a pine tree.
Best week of my life.
-KERBY LODGE GUEST BOOK-

In my neck of the woods, tourism is a very big deal. Several area colleges have stellar hotel management programs to meet the growing demand.

When I contacted them to find a summer intern, however, I was informed that students prefer jobs in the Bahamas and Florida. At fancy resorts with uniforms and nametags, and shiny brass luggage carts.

Not at falling-apart family lodges with Lincoln Log cabins in the woods.

There hasn't been a luggage cart invented that can navigate the bumpy tree roots lining the walkways of Kerby Lodge. Or over the hard acorns that can twist your ankles. Just one of the unique charms my lodge boasts.

One instructor confessed that lodges such as mine are barely touched upon in the curriculum. He called Kerby Lodge an "outlier"—right up there with yurt villages, and *glamping*.

Hollis Fanning must herself be an outlier. A third-year student at Michigan State University, she seemed excited about the internship. Maybe too excited. But I wasn't about to talk her out of it.

Hollis *loves* Lake Michigan, she gushed during our phone interview.

She loves rustic lodges. And fishing. And organizing things. Puppies, and kittens, and big fluffy snowflakes too, I imagined. I could only hope she'd feel the same about racoons, falling tree branches, and rusty water pipes.

A big plus was that her parents would be at their cottage close by. Knowing that Hollis came with emergency grown-ups helped calm the anxiety I felt at leaving my business in her young, enthusiastic hands.

I reminded myself that I was close to Hollis' age when I inherited the lodge. And I turned out to be more capable than some gave me credit for—eventually, anyway.

So, I hoped, would Hollis Fanning.

But could Kerby Lodge run without me?

Did it?

I wrestled with these thoughts during various stages of sleep and wakefulness after returning home. The lodge was just starting to run with me for the first time in 13 years. Last summer was the first peak season that I took real ownership of my resort and all its potential. The first time I applied myself to its success.

And instead of building on the momentum, what do I do? Run halfway around the world with the first devastatingly handsome man who asked me to marry him.

To eat schnitzel, and strudels.

And those little pots of melted cheese, with hunks of dark brown bread to dip.

"Kaker, Kaker…"

As in a dream, I could hear Luke's voice.

"Nnn," I said in response.

"You slept all day yesterday, Kaker," he said, "you should get up."

"I will," I tried to say. To my ears, it sounded like, "ah wahhh."

He reached down and kissed me on the cheek, and then left. Presumably, for work. As vice principal of the middle school, Luke had to report weeks sooner than us humble substitute teachers. The delicious clean scent of his soap followed him out of the room.

Come back, I thought, reaching out a limp hand and catching only air.

Did I really sleep all day yesterday? No wonder I was starving. Jennifer left us cheese and crackers, and orange juice. But the last real meal I remember eating was on the airplane.

Ick.

Dozing off again, I shook myself awake. This jet lag was hitting me like a ton of bricks, but I had to fight it. I had barely moved since we got home. Except to take the occasional sip of juice, nibble a cracker, and look to see if Lake Michigan was still there.

Then stumble back to bed.

With eyes still closed, I forced my brain to engage in the world around me. I could feel the summer breeze on my skin, and the sun on my face. The sound of laughter, and the scent of coconut sunscreen, came up from the beach through the open window.

My mind could picture the bright sky and brighter bathing suits.

On the other end of my body, my foot throbbed with a dull ache—why was that?

I quickly remembered. In the dark, I stubbed my toes hard on boxes stacked in an unexpected location. Trying not to wake Luke, I shook my fists in an exaggerated pantomime until the pain subsided. In the early morning light I saw I had no one to blame but myself.

"Ugh," I said out loud, "wedding gifts." The wedding gifts I'd meant to unpack for the past year. The gifts that suddenly had nowhere else to go.

Texts may be left to interpretation, but boxes don't lie.

While the lodge and A-Frame were both in one piece, it was apparent that something had gone terribly wrong. More than one thing. Yet, nobody had called me. I mulled this over, willing my leaden arms and legs to move.

When did we land, two days ago? Three?

Dragging myself out of bed, I stumbled to the shower. I needed to get back to the business of the inn. There were cabins to fill. There were trees to cut down. Plus, I had mysteries to solve. What did Hollis' texts mean? Why were Daniel's boxes in the apartment?

And most importantly, what has Luke been eating—and did he bring me anything?

4

The jury is out on all your changes.
Staying in our favorite cabin before you gentrify it.
-KERBY LODGE GUEST BOOK-

"Could the girls come in August?"

My brother Tad called me four weeks ago from Atlanta. I had one foot out the door for our trip, and was surprised by his question.

Theodore Kerby, an orthopedic surgeon, had a medical conference in Vancouver, and his wife Selby decided to join him. Afterwards, they'd sightsee, and tour the area.

"Bella and Wren are excited about spending a month at Kerby Lodge," Tad said.

My head nodded when he said this, but my mind asked: *Are they really?* The girls had never shown interest in spending time here. And why now— why would Bella want to come here for any part of her last high school summer?

I should have asked. Instead, I said "Yes, yes… of course!"

Ever the eager-to-please little sister.

And now, it was the thought of teenagers coming that shot a wake-up call of adrenaline through my sleepy veins. My two nieces were arriving in just days, and I didn't feel anywhere near ready.

12

Luke thought it was brilliant. He himself would be away for most of August at conferences, and was glad I wouldn't be alone.

I know how to be alone, I thought, but didn't say.

"They can help you run the resort," Luke told me, "and get a taste for what it's like to be a Kerby at Kerby Lodge."

That thought did make me happy.

Long ago, there were seven Kerby's that ran the business each summer. Together, we hosted swarms of guests. But Tad left after high school and never looked back. Gram passed away a few years later. Fitz and Raya Kerby, my parents, succumbed to pneumonia 13 years ago. Zeke and June, my aunt and uncle, retired a few years' back.

Leaving me—the last Kerby standing.

And standing I was, though on wobbly, jet-lagged legs.

I opened the apartment refrigerator to find a neatly wrapped turkey and avocado sandwich from the Rusty Nail deli up the road, with a love note on top from Luke.

Eat up Kaker, it read.

It wasn't a love note that would launch a thousand ships. But considering I'd waited 34 years for Mister Right, and hadn't eaten in days, it wooed me like the cover of a drugstore romance—complete with swarthy pirate, and shimmery embossed hearts.

I took my first big bite while leaning against the kitchen sink. Closing my eyes, I chewed and savored the fresh roasted white meat and buttery avocado. The crunchy radish sprouts and tomato slice were a pleasant surprise. Peeking under a corner of the bread, I saw that Luke had them hold the mayo, which nearly brought tears of gratitude to my eyes.

Luke Mayne and I were still strangers to each other in many small ways, yet I trusted him with my heart, my life—and now my sandwiches.

Tentatively, I stepped over to the table and sat down, taking another big bite as I did.

I used to worry about choking when I lived in the lodge alone, but now Hollis and her capable little arms were just yards away, through a sturdy wooden door that led to the dining room. I could hear her talking on the phone to a potential guest about a reservation.

Still, I forced myself to slow down and take much smaller bites.

Taking a deep breath of the fresh air blowing in from the lake, I looked out the open window. My gaze fell on the pines between the lodge and the A-Frame cabin, and I tried to imagine the trees gone.

I hated to cut them down, I really did. But it was the only level spot on the shoreline to place an event tent that would provide shelter for 100 guests, and allow us to be taken seriously as a destination wedding *destination.*

Something I had single-handedly decided Kerby Lodge should be.

The catalyst had been my own wedding reception last September, which had been perfect. The consultant from a destination wedding magazine who attended, thanks to Daniel Mayne and his popular blog, agreed. She was won over by my "authentic rustic amenities."

The Real Deal, she called us in her write-up. "In a world of stuffed brown bears, and lodges with plastic totem poles," she wrote, "Kerby Lodge is the Real Deal."

She loved the twinkling lights in the trees, and the gourmet food-truck feast served on vintage ironstone dishes. The tiered wedding cake baked by my friend Mitch was a hit, with frosted cranberries that replicated the wild berries found in the forest.

And who could not love the images of Luke and I, perched on a low branch of a large white pine as the Lake Michigan sun set behind us. My flowing Irish lace dress puddled softly on the pine needles below; my strawberry blond hair shone against the red sky.

And Luke… *Luke!* Looking at me for all the world like a smitten man.

Her photographer captured stunning images that made it into the magazine, generating a ton of interest. Before I knew it, I was over-promising to brides like a snake oil salesman.

"Yes, I will have an event tent," I heard myself saying. "Very soon."

Because as beautiful as my property is, I can't guarantee the weather, and I don't have a Plan B, which breaks a cardinal rule found in every wedding magazine:

1. **Only try on dresses within your budget**
2. **Don't get hitched during football season**
3. **Have a backup plan for an outdoor wedding**

The lodge itself can hold 50 guests in bad weather, but is not ideal for the ceremony or reception—the grounds being the true hero. The consultant advised me that the pine forest on the bluff overlooking Lake Michigan was the perfect spot.

She said that if I managed to stage a few wedding photos with a tent by mid-September, I could have an ad in the winter issue of *Destination Wedding, Lake Michigan.* Then I could capitalize on not one, but two full wedding seasons. Because area couples getting engaged over the Christmas holidays will rely on the winter issue of *DW, LM* for every decision.

"Every. Decision." She said, leaving no doubt about its importance.

The deadline is ambitious. And I'm beginning to realize that the tent is the tip of the iceberg—I'll also need more parking, facilities for caterers and florists, and probably a few other things. But it will be worth it when that first bride spends her lovely budget at Kerby Lodge.

"You want to go to all that trouble?" Luke solemnly asked me.

"I do," I vowed.

5

At the lake, we don't hide CRAZY.
We parade it on the beach and give it a cocktail.
-KERBY LODGE GUEST BOOK-

"Good morning Hollis," I said, coffee in hand.

How I'd missed the shiny new coffee pot in the Kerby Lodge dining room while we were away. I often thought of how smooth that first cup would taste after returning home—milder than the strong shots of espresso we had experienced in our travels.

My stomach fluttered happily at the cookies next to the urn, and I put two on a napkin.

I'd placed an ad offering a paid summer internship, and Hollis Fanning, my one applicant, was destined for the job. She was perky in a way that made me cringe a little. But she was prepared, and a hard worker, which I respected.

While in Europe, I compared her energy level to the desk clerks that greeted us at our various inns, and she won every time. Even without the home court advantage of lederhosen.

She was compact in her summer dress, and efficient in all her movements. And cute in a way I envied. I had always wanted to be cute, but was too lanky—even as a baby.

I imagined other mothers looking into my stroller and telling Raya, "Oh, well, isn't she…" as they scrambled for a nice word.

Isn't she *something*.

Doesn't she look *competent*.

"Kay," Hollis bubbled as she spun around to face me, "it's two in the afternoon!"

She appeared very much at home in the dining room of the lodge, my dining room, where she had set up a little desk in the bay window that overlooked the driveway. Here, she could see guests come and go. Why hadn't I thought of that? It was the perfect location. Further, it freed up my previous desk: the kitchen table in the apartment.

Pulling out a dining chair, I sat down like an uninvited guest. I could no longer loom over Hollis' tiny stature, feeling for all the world like a moose by comparison.

On the computer screen, I could see that Hollis was entering data into the ledger software that I'd purchased, but hadn't installed. Next to the desk, she had a whiteboard where she had drawn the weather forecast for the day in bright washable markers.

The smiling sun looked a lot like Hollis herself.

Not wanting to be the raincloud, I forced myself to smile.

"Really. Afternoon!" I was genuinely surprised.

"Welcome home, regardless," Hollis said.

I nodded, and took a drink. The coffee I had missed so much was bitter and cold. I pretended it was wonderful, and nibbled a cookie. In cooler months, there would be a fresh pot at all times. But summer guests rarely wanted afternoon coffee on such warm days.

A man walked into the dining room just then, and ignored me while saying hello to Hollis. "Hi Ken," Hollis said, transferring all of her attention, "how was the fishing?"

"Great!" he said, "I went to that spot you suggested, and caught a beautiful brown trout. The filets are out in the angler's ice chest. I'll take them home tomorrow."

"Sounds good Ken," Hollis replied, "your sandwich is in the wine cooler."

Since when did we have an *angler's ice chest* or a *wine cooler*, and… sandwich?

By answer, Hollis turned to me and said "The Rusty Nail gives me free delivery. I call in lunch orders, and they deliver by noon. It's very popular with my guests. Because no one," she said, "wants to leave the beach on a sunny day like today."

This last part wasn't news to me—I'd lived at a vacation lodge my entire life.

"I label and place the lunches in the indoor wine cooler for pickup, and everyone is delighted," she went on. "It enhances the customer experience."

She said *customer experience* very slowly. As if she were teaching me a term that I would be tested on later. I bristled.

And did she really say *my guests*?

"Hollis, is the wine cooler you've been mentioning the actual refrigerator that's right here in this room? The old beat-up fridge that's always been here?" I asked.

She waited until Ken retreated, then told me she thought it was a "tad bit gross" to use the same fridge for both worms and wine, so she split them up. The anglers now put their bait and fish filets in an even older refrigerator out in the shed, next to the oars.

Hollis told me how she evicted the worms, then gave the guest fridge in the lodge a thorough scrubbing, and added a cute sign that read *Wine and Cheese, No Worms Please*.

My foggy brain raced to keep up as she went on about a magnetic holder she stuck on the fridge. Something about colorful papers and pens that she uses to label lunches—art supplies that guests can use to mark their drinks and snacks.

Again, why didn't I think of that?

Looking into the old fridge when Ken opened it, I could see it was clean and organized. And what I should have said was "great work," instead of the small and petty words that came out of my mouth.

"Kerby Lodgers have never confused worms with wine before," I remarked.

Hollis gave me an indulgent look as she continued entering data. We both knew her idea was good. *Real* good.

I tucked a cookie in my mouth.

"Hey," I said minutes later, around a mouthful of oats, "have you seen Luke?"

"He left early to check in at the school," she said.

"How is he not jetlagged?" I asked out loud, though not really looking for an answer.

Hollis smiled and tilted her head at the crumbs gathering on my shirt. "Luke probably avoided salty snacks, fatty foods, and sugary beverages."

Before my slow brain could react, Hollis politely asked me about our trip, and I gave her some of the highlights. Seconds later, when her eyes started glazing over, I asked her how everything went for the inn while I was away.

"Great—no probs," she said, as I took another sip of my cold coffee. Still bitter.

No probs is ideal, I thought, but remembered the cryptic messages.

18

"Then maybe you can explain the texts."

"You're just like my mom," Hollis said. "She doesn't understand texts either."

I flinched at the comparison.

"Here's one Hollis," I said, scrolling through my phone, "*Grt Rm BRNT dwn.*"

She looked into space for a minute. "Oh right," she said at last. "The burnt orange sofa in the great room—I wondered if it had down-filled cushions. I wanted to have them cleaned."

"Wow, that makes perfect sense in a crazy sort of way," I exclaimed. "I thought the great room burned down."

"You did *not!*" Hollis said, smiling broadly as if I'd said something very funny.

"How about this one?" I asked, "5 HURT in fall."

"Barb Hurt wants a bigger cabin in October," she said, "one that sleeps five."

Taking a deep breath, I allowed my tense muscles to relax.

I had cracked Hollis' code—her messages were nothing but benign misunderstandings.

"Then Fld A FRM could only mean there was a flood of interest for renting the A-Frame cabin this summer." By this point I was smiling myself.

"Well, no Kay," Hollis said, her smile quickly fading.

"A pipe burst in the A-Frame and water sprayed everywhere," she said. "Daniel was away, and it went on for two days. The sub-floor was destroyed."

My mouth hung open as I stared at Hollis, speechless.

"The kitchen island was totaled, along with the furniture," Hollis continued, "as the text clearly said."

"Clearly," I said.

6

No more "moldy oldy" lodge.
I guess that's why you raised the rates.
-KERBY LODGE GUEST BOOK-

I took a brisk walk to the empty and echoing A-Frame to confirm what Hollis said—and could see for myself that a spewing pipe had wreaked havoc on the main floor of the cabin.

It must have happened soon after Luke and I left, because the kitchen island had been rebuilt already, and primer covered the damaged walls. Everywhere I looked, new sub-flooring was nailed down where contractors had removed the old tile.

The water damage explained Daniel's boxes—he must have hastily moved his stuff to the apartment, thinking it wouldn't be in anyone's way. He couldn't have predicted that on the other end of my vast property, Gram's house would also need major repairs.

These cabins were getting old, and the lodge was even older. I would have to factor more repairs into my already hefty maintenance budget, I realized with a heavy sigh.

After getting over the initial shock, I could admit that while the damages were painful and costly, the changes looked promising. With all the harvest gold linoleum in the dumpster, new flooring would be an improvement.

I wondered what my interior decorators were envisioning for this vast, vaulted space. They had steered me towards a bamboo flooring for Gram's house—sleek planks with the look of beautiful hardwood, and a bullet-proof finish.

The practicality of which could not be underestimated.

For decades, people had been coming in and out of the Kerby Lodge cabins with sand on their feet and shoes, and more sand falling off their

20

bathing suits and beach towels. Sandblasting every surface they came into contact with.

I'm sure that's why my parents left the ancient wine-colored carpet in the lodge itself, instead of exposing the beautiful heart pine flooring that was cowering underneath.

Gazing at the brown paneled walls of the A-Frame, soaring up at an angle to the loft, I tried to picture how they would look painted our chosen shade of Irish Lace white. Beautiful, no doubt. A fresh coat on everything would make it seem better, and brighter. As it had in every cottage we'd updated so far.

Even more beautiful was the thought of contractors with scaffolding tackling these tall walls, instead of me.

Even so, I didn't like being surprised upon my return, and a feeling of betrayal settled in my stomach like a rock. Followed by a wave of exhaustion.

I plopped down on the floor in the middle of the A-Frame, expelling the air out of my lungs. Then I closed my eyes and inhaled. The smell of the new wood reminded me of when my dad had the cabin built—I must have been three or four years old. He would often bring me to the site, making it seem as if we were going on an adventure.

We would hike through the grove of pine trees. The same trees I planned to remove.

"Look, Kaker, there it is!" Fitz would have me peek around one of the pines as he pointed excitedly, "Mummy's secret cabin."

I'd laugh with my dad, and clap my hands.

While Dad worked away crafting the rough-hewn stairs, I would play and nap on a worn quilt under a shade tree. Counting the sailboats gliding along the lake, I'd fall asleep on the sun-warmed blanket to the sounds of Dad's sander, and the waves gently splashing in the distance.

Dad had the A-Frame built as a retreat for Raya. But as Kerby legend goes, a family from Chicago called just as it was finished, requesting a cabin for a two-week vacation. They wanted their boys to be able to run and play in the woods, and canoe and sail every day.

"We can 'nae say nae!" Raya had passionately brogued to Fitz—the fate of a city family in desperate need of a swim sitting squarely in her hands.

And so, veering from its original intention, Fitz and Raya rented the brand-new A-Frame to Nan and Sperry Mayne and their sons, Daniel and Luke. Without any idea that, years later, the Mayne brothers would return to Kerby Lodge as grown men.

My parents had no way of knowing that by saying *aye* to the Mayne's so many years ago, they would completely change our family history.

Daniel would come back and save my inn.

Luke would soon follow and save my life.

And now, gazing up at the vaulted loft bedroom, it occurred to me that once upon a time, my parents had met and talked with Nan and Sperry—my in-laws. And surely had even seen Luke, my future husband, playing on the grounds and in the woods near the lodge.

Och, there's a fine, handsome lad—did Raya think this? Did she get a quickening in her heart as she gazed out her window at Luke? Did he stand out from the other boys?

It's likely that my dad helped the Mayne brothers pull the little boats and canoes into the water in the early hours of morning. Daniel once told me that he and Luke would slip out before their parents were awake, and have great adventures in the woods and water.

"Now, these are good boys," my dad might have said to himself; "the kind of boys that grow into good men—the kind of men I'd like my Kaker to marry someday."

My heart felt warm.

Even loose threads, I realized, could hold important things together.

There was no denying that the A-Frame renovations were much needed. But they had been on the bottom of my priority list. One reason was that my brother-in-law had unofficially claimed this as his base camp between freelance design gigs. And after all the help he'd given me the winter before last, with renovating the lodge and rejuvenating my business, letting Daniel come and go seemed to be the least I could do.

The downside was that the cabin was off the books as an income generator. Which is the reason, I gathered, Hollis didn't consider it one of her "probs" while I was away.

And now there would be a new dilemma. The A-Frame would be ready in time for the busy fall color season, and could make Kerby Lodge a lot of money before we closed up for winter. This income potential was not a small thing.

But evicting Daniel was not a small thing either. Not as easy as evicting a winter mouse, or even a family of raccoons. Those, I could do in my sleep.

"So... I can't believe you didn't call me!"

Before I could check the feelings of frustration and betrayal welling up inside of me, I took them for a walk—right into Carriage House Treasures. "You didn't think to call and tell me about the flooded A-Frame, or the leak in Gram's house?"

What should have been a warm greeting between me and one of my oldest friends quickly transgressed as the edge in my voice escalated.

"Hello to you too," Jennifer Jansen said, in a cool response. "Welcome home."

As an EMT professional, Jennifer had literally become a lifesaver when a reclusive lodger, my now brother-in-law, injured himself on my property over a year ago. Since then, she has become a business partner by setting up her shop in my once neglected carriage house.

"I'm sorry Jen," I said, not sounding the slightest bit sorry. "I am just surprised to be learning about my crumbling inn now, instead of when the damages occurred."

"Hollis said she texted you," Jennifer said, calmly.

"I had my phone off," I jabbed back at her.

"How was I to know that?" She asked, reasonably, I suppose.

"I expected you to phone whatever inn we were at," I said, "in an emergency."

Jennifer gazed at me with the eagle eye of a medical professional, assessing me—and it infuriated me. My face was probably red as a beet under her stare.

"I don't think of a leaky pipe as an emergency, Kay," she said.

Of course she didn't—in her world, "emergency" had a far graver meaning.

"And look how upset you are," Jennifer continued. "Imagine how this news would have ruined your vacation. There was nothing you could have done from Italy..."

"France!" I practically shouted.

"Or France," she said, calmly.

Jennifer went on to tell me that she had contacted my Uncle Zeke, who called the insurance agent. It's what I would have asked her to do.

"Your insurance is paying for most of the repairs on both buildings Kay," Jennifer was saying, "and your return timing is perfect. You can choose paint colors and flooring."

I nodded in agreement.

Jennifer was trying to assuage my bad temper, I knew. But at some point, it was I who would need to apologize for my behavior—the same bad behavior that ruined any chance of catching up with my old friend.

As she placed her WELCOME sign out for customers, it was clearly not for me. There was no "Feel Free to Browse" for Kay Kerby Mayne, if the sparks in Jen's eyes were any indication.

I mustered up the last of my bad temper and huffed and puffed back to the lodge.

At least I had new furniture all ready to go, and my mother-in-law Nan would be delighted. A devout follower of Daniel's design blog, she had brought her old sunroom furniture for the A-Frame when they came to our wedding reception last year. And by "old," it was pristine. She may have lightly perched on it once or twice, with the delicacy of a tiny bird.

Nan asks me often if I've swapped the old furniture for the new yet.

"Pieces in a puzzle," I tell her, and it's the truth.

I didn't want to put her pretty furniture in such an outdated room. "Once the old stuff is out, I'll need to paint the walls and probably the cupboards, too. I should replace the old flooring. And so on, and so on," I have said to Nan, more than once.

Pieces in a costly, time-consuming puzzle that I wanted to put off indefinitely.

But thanks to a burst pipe, everything would be falling into place by the end of summer. If I had replaced the furniture any sooner, it would be Nan's pieces we'd be throwing out!

I love it when procrastination pays off.

7

*A bad day of fishing is still better
Than a good day of working*
-KERBY LODGE GUEST BOOK-

"This visit needs to be amazing."

I declared this to Hollis as I walked into the lodge dining room days later.

"Of course it does," she replied.

"When I left for Europe, we still had cabins available in August, right?"

Hollis looked up from her desk and took in my pathetic face. After being home for nearly a week, I still hadn't shaken the jet lag.

"Yes, we had lots of open cabins when you left," Hollis said, nodding and smiling.

After all the hard work we had put into promoting my lodge, the phones were ringing and the new scheduling system was great. But we weren't at capacity this summer. It shouldn't have made me happy, but at this moment in time, it did.

I mirrored Hollis' smile, and exhaled with relief.

Though I had done my best, the apartment was hopeless. The solution was to move Bella, Wren, and myself into one of the cabins that Jack and Stace had renovated, I told Hollis, or move to one of the older chalets. Anything would be nicer than the crowded apartment.

But then she shocked me by saying, "There were openings, but now we're booked. There are no availabilities at all this summer."

"What... ?" I stammered.

It seems I had no sooner left her in charge, when Hollis registered the inn with VeRoom.com, the trending website for last minute travelers. Now, every room and cabin at Kerby Lodge was fully booked.

"The profit margin is slightly lower," Hollis said, "but we make up for that in volume."

Ingenious.

I wanted to strangle her.

Suddenly, I was no different from the hundreds of women who had called Kerby Lodge over the years, desperately seeking a larger cabin, a closer cabin, or a different week. Anything that would allow their family to enjoy a Lake Michigan vacation before returning to the daily grind of work and school.

The grind of driving their mother-in-law to a weekly hair appointment, and cleaning up after the neighbor's dog. Of being a non-stop taxi service to kids and their friends. Of being volun*told* to bring cupcakes to a class party. Of finding the time to assemble yet another tuna noodle casserole with a potato chip topping, to be eaten by an unappreciative family.

These moms just wanted one week when the kids could make their own baloney sandwiches, sleep in their bathing suits, and play outside from dawn to dusk. One week where they themselves might read a book, and lay in the sun.

Mum allowed me to field many of these calls, but I never appreciated their desperation as much as I did right now. Time was running out. I'd be leaving for the airport in a few short days, and the best I'd managed to do was carve a path to the bunk beds in Tad's old room by moving boxes around and stacking them higher.

"But, that's great news, isn't it?" Luke was asking over dinner. "Kerby Lodge hasn't been completely booked in years." He would be leaving soon for the first of his two conferences.

"Yes, Pollyanna, it's great," I said.

Luke laughed, but I didn't.

When I told Hollis to make herself at home while I was away, I never realized she'd take it literally, and disband anything she found archaic, unprofitable, or "a tad bit gross." This perky little steamroller partnered with VeRoom.com, swapped incandescent lightbulbs for efficient LEDs, and changed our laundry schedule to align with lower utility rates.

She renegotiated our utilities, took over the social media accounts, and retired a battered old ice machine that was draining electricity—sending it to the curb on dumpster day.

She alphabetized and digitized all my contacts and communications.

26

Set up an account with the Rusty Nail.

She even got the housekeepers to consent to an efficiency study.

Yet, all I could focus on was my inconvenience. "But Luke," I said, disheartened, "staying in the cramped apartment is not how I envisioned my visit with the girls."

I imagined the three of us smiling and laughing—taking early morning swims, and gliding in kayaks along the quiet water. Sitting by the bonfire and watching sunsets. Spending rainy afternoons catching up on our summer reading.

We would cook together, and share secrets.

In the evenings, we'd drink warm tea and cocoa, and look through old photos of Kerby Lodge—one of the boxes from Gram's house contained pictures, I was sure. Of course, the girls would want to hear all the old stories.

August would fly by, and the girls would cry when they had to go home. "There, there," I'd reassure them, "you can come back any time."

"Bella and Wren are Kerby's, and Kerby chicks are tough," Luke interrupted my wandering thoughts to say. "You can do everything you want to during the day, and still sleep in the apartment at night."

I nodded reluctantly as I gazed up at this handsome man, wishing we were back in France, sipping espressos at Michelin-starred restaurants.

I'd hardly seen Luke since we got home, and we were out of sync. He left early in the mornings, and I could barely stay awake past dinner. I'd gotten used to having Luke by my side, and felt shaky at the thought of him leaving.

"Have a great time," he said. "I will be home before you know it, Kaker Mayne."

8

Good Times and Tan Lines
On the beautiful Kerby Lodge beach.
-KERBY LODGE GUEST BOOK-

Nobody in my family calls me Kay.

They have called me Kaker since I was just a toddler and tried to say Kay Kerby. For a while there, "Kakers" were few and far between. But since our wedding a year ago, I'm surrounded by family.

My groom delights in saying "Kaker Mayne," which speeds up my heartrate significantly.

Daniel, my tall, dark, and brooding brother-in-law, started calling me Kaker in earnest on the day of the wedding reception, as he reprised his role as Luke's best man. And *Och*, wouldn't my dear Mum, the poetic Raya Kerby, have loved Daniel's toast.

"To the marriage of Luke and Kaker Mayne," he said, raising his glass.

"May your life be long and happy, your cares and sorrows few,
may the many friends around you prove faithful, fond and true..."

There was more, something about *wedding cake... unsalted lake...* all I remember was the rare show of emotion from this otherwise stoic man, who had come to be so important in my life. I wasn't sure how I felt about Daniel's girlfriend Francine, but come to think of it, she hasn't been around all that much.

28

Then, neither have I.

Of course, Aunt June and Uncle Zeke always call me Kaker on the phone from Florida. My in-laws from Chicago do as well. Only, Nan says *Kakah* in her broad Boston accent. I confess that sometimes I call her for no other reason.

I'll always be Kaker to my brother Tad, and his wife Selby is getting on board too. We are all much closer since they came up for our wedding party, and after Luke and I went south to spend Christmas with the Atlanta Kerby's.

It was the most time my brother and I have had together since we were kids—except for the tragic weeks we spent a dozen years ago, settling our parents' estate.

"It's good to make new memories," I told Tad, as we sat by the Christmas tree in his historic home on the Beltway. We had been sipping coffee with peppermint creamer, and nibbling on southern delicacies that included ham biscuits, cheese straws and pimento spread.

How did Selby and the other southern belles keep their figures?

As surprising as it was that the girls were coming to visit, it was Tad promising he and Selby would stay at Kerby Lodge for a few days when they came back that shocked me. It would be Labor Day weekend—the last few glorious days of summer before the shoulder season.

Through the years, the stubborn, willful absence of Tad had co-mingled in my heart with the loss of our parents, until I found it impossible to distinguish between the two sad emotions. But it wasn't too late for Tad. He could still be a part of Kerby Lodge.

Labor Day weekend would be a good start.

As for my nieces, I could only hope that by the end of their summer visit to Kerby Lodge, they would abandon their too formal "Aunt Kay" and call me Kaker instead.

"Families are messy," Hollis had commented when I first told her about their visit.

Slightly taken aback, I reacted too quickly. "I'm sure these girls know how to pick up after themselves," I said, in their defense.

"That's not what I meant," she said, holding my gaze.

Maybe Hollis' cheeky comment was prophetic—my life was starting to feel messy, and the girls' impending arrival wasn't helping. Initially, I was thrilled. But now, I went back and forth between excitement and exhaustion.

I had bitten off a lot this summer.

This morning, as he placed folded shirts in his suitcase, Luke gave a final warning that teens were no different from toddlers. "Don't romanticize them too much," Luke told me. "They will push your buttons and test your limits."

I thought Luke was being over-dramatic, but didn't say so.

Like ships in the night, only in daylight, Luke and the girls would just miss each other at the airport today. My husband would be flying west as Bella and Wren arrived from the south.

"We are going to have so much fun while you're away," I said, half-heartedly, "and even more fun when you get home and join us."

"I will do my part to be fun when I get home, Mrs. Mayne," he said. "Maybe I'll have a home to come home to, and not a bunker." I knew he was referring to the tall stacks of boxes in every room of our temporary quarters.

I tensed at his comment. Wasn't it obvious that I'd rather be in our house too—instead of living out of our luggage in the cramped and cluttered apartment? I certainly didn't want to pick a fight with Luke on his way out the door, but it would have been so easy.

"Hmm," I remained non-committal.

I looked at my tall, handsome husband as he closed and locked his suitcase. He had been a self-proclaimed "nomadic teacher" for all of his adult life—moving from one two-year assignment to the next. And from one two-year apartment lease to the next. He had no idea what it was like to have responsibilities for anything other than his own well-being.

As a single man, he probably took his five shirts to the dry cleaners every week, then stopped at the grocery store for milk, bread, and a rotisserie chicken. He had a simple life with very few complications—until he married me, that is.

A tall, red-haired, non-stop complication.

How could I explain to Luke that in a small coastal town there was an unspoken cadence to the calendar year that affected any project?

For instance, August was a vacation month for just about everyone on and around Lake Michigan—including carpenters, painters, contractors and even decorators. Jack and Stace Wildberry, no doubt, were unashamedly swimming with family at their grandfather's cottage, instead of thinking about my renovations.

We were on their minds, but only socially. They called to invite Luke and I to a cookout, which we had to decline. When we spoke, Stace mentioned that Daniel had already joined them several times, which surprised me. I hadn't known he'd been back in town that much.

But there was very little I could do about the work that had slowed on both the A-Frame and Gram's house during the final weeks of summer.

30

We would all have to wait until family reunions had run their course, a cold front moved in, or the town sold out of hamburger buns.

In the meantime, I had been expanding my Kerby Girls activity list.

Maybe the girls could help Jennifer at the carriage house, or pick up fallen twigs on the massive Kerby property. Bella and Wren are family, not company, I reminded myself.

For fun, we could take a ride out to Wildberry Consignment Shop and see if Beth Wildberry, the owner, had any interesting new pieces.

It was too late to pick cherries and too early to pick apples, but maybe we could catch late season blueberries and do some canning and baking.

They would be a little older—Bella was now 17 and Wren 15 this summer. Two beautiful and fun young Kerby's who would descend on our peak season at the lodge in a swirl of laughter, stories, bikinis, sunglasses and flip flops, and leave just as quickly as they came.

Tanned and happy.

Full of new stories and a love for the lodge and lake that is their heritage. Like lovely summer storms that arrive out of nowhere, and liven up a dull summer afternoon.

9

"Somethin' stinks!"

Bella got out of the car after I found a parking spot on the main street. Her pretty face was twisted into an expression that matched her loud proclamation.

I thought it would be a good idea to grab a bite of lunch before heading to the lodge. This way, the girls could look around the town. Bella, I knew, had her driver's license. She might want to take the Jeep to the library with Wren, or to the Shop and Save to get gum.

Maybe they could meet a few girls from town, and go to the movies together. Or grab an ice cream cone at the Dairy Dip—things I did as a teenager in the summertime.

"Wren?" she asked her sister, "doesn't the air smell like dead fish and worms?"

"Lil' bit," Wren said, in her precious southern drawl.

"The air does *not* stink," I said defensively, feeling tired all of a sudden. Someone needed to stick up for the pure Lake Michigan air I loved—an indescribably sweet combination of wind, sand, sunscreen, lemonade, sandwiches, wildflowers and blue skies.

The girls just smiled and looked at each other.

As I walked with them to the Village Diner, I thought about how much they had changed since Christmas. A few months ago, they were all fun and politeness for Luke and I. Was it because they were with their watchful parents then?

Now, it seems, Bella had packed some sass for this trip—and not the travel size.

Her greeting at the airport was cool, and I overcompensated by being effusive and too eager. At the luggage pickup, she pointed to her gigantic suitcase on the conveyor belt with manicured nails, then turned to look at her phone. Leaving me to make a mad grab for it.

I'm still kicking myself.

The girls stopped to look in a boutique as I went ahead to get a table.

"Take your time," I said, glad to see smiles on their faces.

I grabbed a booth by the window, and ordered a cold Coke—unsure what the girls were drinking. After a full ten minutes, and after the waiter refilled my drink once, the girls still hadn't joined me. Looking out, I could see a group of teens on the sidewalk, and was surprised that Bella and Wren were among them.

I took a good look at them for the first time since I'd picked them up.

Both girls were wearing bright white sandals and short white shorts. Bella wore a buttery yellow tee shirt with an Auburn University logo on the front, and delicate gold jewelry. The yellows complemented her straight chestnut hair and creamy complexion.

Wren was slightly taller than Bella, though just as willowy. Wren's hair was nearly as red as her grandmother Raya's, and she wore a sleeveless oxford in Loden green—my own color of choice, though my hair was more strawberry blonde than fiery red.

I tapped on the window, and Bella gave me a practiced "one minute" signal with her pretty pink nail—barely looking up to see if it was me.

"How do they do that?" I said quietly to myself—they'd been in town mere minutes, and were already standing with a group of rich kids in popped collars and boat shoes. It's as if they all recognize and gravitate to their own kind.

I have always felt outside of this particular *kind*—at least for three hot months of every year. That's when our sleepy lakeshore town would be inundated with tourists, day-trippers, and cottage owners. Endless crowds of people demanding to be lodged and fed and catered to.

There would be grown men raising their voices because our little food store doesn't sell the *Wall Street Journal*, grown women throwing tantrums because there's no valet parking at the beach, and the kids they conceived.

Kids who, for years, have looked just like the group outside the Village Diner.

They were a fickle bunch, the summer kids. They'd feign friendship one minute, if it suited their purpose, then snicker behind our backs after we served them ice cream at the Dairy Dip, or cleared their dishes at the yacht club.

It's no wonder many of my classmates wanted to blend in during the summer crush of wealthy tourists—I don't blame any of them for trying. My friends would save their babysitting and lawn mowing money to buy one or two of the expensive boutique shirts, or a pair of deck shoes, but could not convincingly imitate the confidence possessed by the summer kids.

As I got older, I began to realize that our parents sat on land and businesses valued at millions of dollars, and were often worth more than the people we tirelessly served all summer.

Still, I didn't look forward to reliving any part of my own teenaged years, through the experiences of Bella and Wren. But I needn't have worried. Looking out the window, I saw a new generation of Kerby's—completely at ease in the presence of the summer kids, if not owning the group outright.

Bella and Wren were daughters of a successful surgeon and an Atlanta socialite with old money. They were raised to ride Arabian horses and play stringed instruments, and to aspire to Ivy League schools.

With their sweet southern drawls, they were a refreshing novelty to this mostly Midwest group. "Y'all are so sweet to be so nice to my *lil' sister* and I..." I heard Bella say through a screened window in the diner. She was laying it on thick.

I could see this pack sniffing out my nieces—their education, their causes and their confidence—and wordlessly declaring them "one of us."

It was like watching a National Geographic cable program on migratory birds, or the introduction of wolves back into Yellowstone.

In their world, I knew, I would be at the bottom of the pecking order.

Me, with a master's degree in education, twelve acres of land, and prime Lake Michigan frontage. I was still, in Miss Austen's economy, a shopkeeper and not a Fudgie—what the locals in Lake Michigan towns call the tourists, on account of the many fudge shops that are famous with the visitors.

And it was true, I was not here on vacation.

I was here to make a living.

Looking outside again, Bella was standing close to, and laughing with, one of the boys in the group. He had bleached blonde hair and was wearing a faded blue oxford shirt. His scuffed and battered leather boat shoes likely cost one hundred dollars, but looked as though he rescued them this morning from the dog's mouth.

He and Bella had their cell phones pulled out and seemed to be exchanging phone numbers. A wave of panic coursed through me.

Who was this boy?

Tapping again on the window, a little harder this time, I mouthed the word *NOW* in such an exaggerated way as not to be misunderstood. Inadvertently, getting everyone's attention, and probably embarrassing the girls.

We were all quiet on the way home after eating our burgers. Except for Bella commenting to Wren that at least there would be *something* to do this summer, now that they had met Max and his friends.

Max, I gathered, was the boy with the bleached blonde hair.

I had not considered that there would be boys to contend with while Bella and Wren were visiting. Should I call Tad and Selby, and ask them the ground rules?

Sheesh, I only had them for two hours, and I was in over my head.

What else am I not prepared for?

As if she read my mind, Wren said, in a southern drawl that could have been her mother's voice, "You don't have to worry about me this summer, Aunt Kay. I'll just be *swimmin'* in Lake Michigan. Imagine—*swimmin'* in such a big safe lake, with no salt and no sharks."

I nodded distractedly, still thinking about the boy in town.

I wasn't so sure about the sharks.

10

If my boss calls, take a message.
Take it to the bonfire and throw it in!
-KERBY LODGE GUEST BOOK-

The Great Lakes are a bit like my nieces—breathtakingly beautiful, but it's a mistake to think they are tame, or safe. And I suspect it's the currents you don't see that are the most dangerous.

Lake Michigan's waves can reach twenty feet high or higher. With miles of sand beaches, it has double the deaths per year of the other great lakes combined. But while the waves are dangerous, it's the riptides that are deadly.

Once I heard it said that people who are drowning in Lake Michigan don't call out for help. Instead, they quietly go under after being pulled out into deep water.

No one has ever drowned at Kerby Lodge, thankfully.

Some think that our beach is immune because of the cove we are nestled in. But where there are waves, there are currents and undertows. We do have a measure of protection from the sand bar, however. And the arms of land that jut out on either side of the cove breaks the fetch of the wind that causes the powerful waves and pulls.

My dad, the engineer, taught me that "fetch" referred to the distance wind travels before something stops it—like the shore or dunes. And a "full fetch" often means high winds and dangerous conditions.

My mother, the Scot, taught me that there's a haunting poem for every occasion, and Lake Michigan storms are no exception. Watching the gusts from the safety of the great room, she'd say *Och Kaker, it's a full fetch o' the wind this day.*

Before reciting something by Robert Burns.

The wind and waves incorporated themselves into my dreams as I napped, the day after returning to the lodge with my nieces. There was a warm breeze buffeting the screened-in window when I lay down on my bed in the apartment.

It was a huge disappointment that I could not host the girls at the newly refinished house—their great grandmother's house. Or even in one of the roomier chalets.

Instead, we all had to squeeze into this apartment, where every room was a jumbled mess. And all my idealized images of being an easy breezy effortless host had likewise dissipated in a puddle of goo.

We were off to a rocky start, the girls and I, but today I was almost too tired to care. They seemed less than thrilled with the little town, and were clearly not happy with their accommodations.

"What *is* this place?" Bella asked me when I showed them to the bunk room. In spite of consolidating the boxes as best as I could, and making up the beds with fresh clean linens and spreads, it still looked like a storeroom.

"It's your dad's old room, Bella," I said, "it's where he grew up."

Try it, I thought, but didn't say.

This morning, I woke up feeling better than I had in weeks. But when my nieces finally rolled out of the bunks, I heard them bickering over the closet space they had to share and the small bathroom, and complaining loudly about the tight spaces and mildew smell in the shower.

They definitely took the wind out of my sails.

At breakfast, one of the girls saw a tiny ant on the window sill and declared that my vintage kitchen was not a fit place to eat. Nibbling my toast, I took a good look at them. "Weren't you both here last September for my reception? Why are you shocked and appalled that Kerby Lodge is not the Hilton?"

Wren answered by reminding me they stayed in the cute, newly renovated cottage with the black and cream wing chairs, and fresh paint. And that everything in and around the lodge and property had been decked out for the party.

"Yeah," Bella chimed in. "Daddy showed us this apartment, but it wasn't so junky. It was cute, like a little museum. Like a tiny settler's cabin on the prairie we once saw out West."

I nodded, taking it all in as the girls gingerly put their dishes in the sink, being careful not to be attacked by the tiny little ant.

There would be no baking or canning today.

Somehow, we got through the morning. I asked the girls if they would like to order a sandwich from the Rusty Nail. They gladly accepted and went to find Hollis.

Hollis Fanning showed no sign of leaving her post at the lodge desk, and I showed no desire to rise up and reclaim my rightful place as proprietor. Frankly, she was proficient. Also, I was unwilling to give up my afternoon naps—a habit I developed in Europe, and brought back with me. Like a wonderful souvenir.

I ordered a sandwich myself.

Thanks to Hollis' new arrangement with VeRoom.com I could pay my intern, order expensive lunches, and still make a healthy profit.

Later, I left the girls sitting on the burnt orange sofa in the great room, flipping through their phones, and went to lie down. I slept hard and deep. And soon, I found myself dreaming about the fetch of the wind.

In my dream, guests were happily swimming in the Lake Michigan sunshine, but then sudden dark clouds appeared, and walls of wind came out of nowhere. I walked out on the sun porch and tried to warn the swimmers, but no sound came out of my mouth.

I could hear people screaming.

From where I stood in my dream, I could actually see the wind bouncing hard off the shore and creating a rip tide that pulled guests out too deep. They screamed, and there was nothing I could do about it. My limbs were like lead and I couldn't move. I fought with my arms and legs, and tried to call out to my guests.

I was trying to save them.

When I did manage at last to cry out, I woke myself up—then realized I was in my bed, tangled in the summer blanket. But through the open window I heard shouts and screams that made me wonder if somebody might really be in trouble!

Staggering out of bed before fully waking, I rushed to the sunlit window only to trip over a stack of boxed-up wedding gifts that were blocking my route. I held my leg and cried out. After regaining my composure and drying my tears, I felt a goose egg-sized lump on my shin, and fought to stand up.

There, in Lake Michigan, I could see Bella and Wren shouting and laughing in the clear blue water as they splashed and climbed on and off an inflatable raft. Splashing and laughing alongside them was Max—the boy they met in town. I could see his jet ski bobbing in the water, anchored near the sand bar.

The sun was clearly shining, yet I couldn't seem to shake the dark clouds that were so real in my dreams.

11

"So lovely was the loneliness of a wild lake,"
Edgar Allan Poe
-KERBY LODGE GUEST BOOK-

No Wedding Gifts

That's what I wanted to say on our invitations last year, but it was vetoed by nearly everyone. My friend and maiden of honor, Jennifer, had the most convincing argument. "One half will bring gifts anyway Kay," she said, "then the other half will feel like dummies."

She pointed out that the "gift nots" would then be running out to the nearest store, which happened to be the Rusty Nail, where they'd stuff last-minute gift baskets with cheeses and ciders. And air-puffed water crackers. The kind I really hated, but ate by the handful anyway, desperately trying to find the flavor.

"That's a lot of baskets," I said.

"And a lot of cheese," Jennifer said.

I knew she was right, and that I shouldn't reinvent the basic social contract of wedding receptions. But I was trying to spare my friends and family—there wasn't anything I actually wanted or needed, and I was zero help when they asked.

What do you give the girl who already has Lake Michigan as her front yard?

A bride who wants nothing more than coffee mugs and dishes that aren't too precious to be left by the bonfire. I really can't have nice things. My kitchen gadgets will end up outside as beach toys or garden tools. My dish towels double as swatters—shooing the occasional fly back out the little kitchen window.

I already had everything.

I had my lake, my lodge and my love.

As for my love, Luke came into our marriage with very little—or so I thought. Just two plush bath towels and a box of plastic eating utensils that were half fork and half spoon. And my heart, which he claimed the moment he arrived at Kerby Lodge.

Last spring, after fielding several lucrative job offers, Luke accepted the role as vice principal for the middle school in my own hometown, without giving me any clue.

In fact, he let me believe he was on his way to Anchorage, Alaska, and then showed up unexpectedly on my doorstep—my doorstep being the rock in the woods where I sat crying my lonely eyes out in the dark.

It was a crisp cool night, and the single finest moment of my life. I realized that Luke Mayne had literally given up a world of opportunities, and moved to my small coastal town to give us a fighting chance. It was far beyond anything I could ever dream.

He proposed to me in the summer, soon after he arrived.

Afterwards, I excitedly took him on a more detailed tour of Kerby Lodge, his new home. I wanted to give him the keys to the kingdom. I wanted him to fall in love with my resort, as much as he had with me. For if anything needed to be loved—for better or for worse, for richer or for poorer—it was my fixer-upper, Kerby Lodge.

As we held hands, we ducked into every unoccupied cabin, and into the apartment, and Gram's house. I then showed him every corner of the rambling lodge itself—the vintage Cape Cod that was a private home long ago, before my parents purchased the 12-acre estate in the early 1970s and turned it into a resort.

On one side of the old lodge is the apartment my parents had carved out of a handful of rooms and the kitchen. On the other side, there's a wing of guestrooms. In the center sits a great room with a big stone fireplace, a dining room, and a massive screened-in porch—all for guests. And two guest apartments upstairs.

Luke knew most of this already. He had been staying in the first guest room, the one with the private bath, since he arrived. It was the same room his brother Daniel stayed in the previous winter, after getting snowed in with me.

Everywhere we went on our giddy tour, I opened cupboards and drawers to reveal the mish-mash of dishes, cast iron fry pans, and jelly jar glasses that I'd grown up with. And yes, I was giddy! I could hardly believe Luke Mayne was at Kerby Lodge at all, after our long-distance friendship had grown into so much more.

I saved the best for the end—the tall stack of beach towels left behind over the course of decades—with faded images of Yogi Bear, the Monkees and Strawberry Shortcake.

"When we're married," I said at the end of the tour, sweeping my arm expansively, "all that's mine will be yours, Luke."

Smiling into my eyes, Luke said, "I pledge thee my sporks, but let's use my towels." Then lifted my hand for a sweet chivalrous kiss.

New towels—that's what I should have asked for!

Instead, I left the decisions up to the gifters. And sadly, the re-gifters.

In addition to generous checks, and thoughtful gift cards, we got sheets for the wrong sized bed, a lava lamp, and an imported mosquito repellent candle, with a sticker that says:

HIGHLY FLAMMABLE, YES!

DO NOT THE USE OF WITHIN PEOPLE, WOOD PAPER.

We got two crockpots—without receipts.

A wall hanging that says: Only Dead Fish Go With The Flow.

And Mayor Peder Maki and his wife Marj gave us a gift card to our favorite place to eat, Mitch's restaurant, as well as a voucher for Marj's knitting class in town—and three skeins of soft ivory wool. Imagining the three-armed sweater I'd no doubt create, I have avoided Marj since the wedding.

"That's what you get when you don't register," my sister-in-law Selby told me following the reception. Her solution was to take most of it to the charity store. Luke suggested that we take the gifts "for a drive, to a farm," where they could run and play with other unwanted gifts.

But I reminded them both that there's a lot of transparency in a small town—people know what gets donated. I wouldn't want to offend anyone. Better to keep them all boxed up and stacked in the apartment, where I can trip over them every night in the dark.

Selby, after being married to my brother Tad for more than 18 years, was finally letting her hair down a bit, I noticed. I even caught her wearing flip flops and a Kerby Lodge sweatshirt while walking to the firepit—after the destination wedding photographer left, of course.

She also told me that every couple needed a few "goofy gifts" to laugh about on those tough days ahead, when conversation was… problematic.

Problematic days?

"That doesn't sound like us at all," I said. "Luke and I have a million things to talk about."

Selby was not convinced.

But so many things were new to both of us. My home town, for one, was new to Luke. I drove him around for days, showing him this beach and that beach, and this road and that road. We went to stores together and bought groceries, chatting all the while about what our favorite foods were, and our strategies for cooking and surviving our busy first weeks in the school system.

We tried all the restaurants in town, and came back to Mitch's time and again for comfort food and fresh fish dinners. Mitch always seemed to have a table by the window for us—as if he were expecting us.

Everywhere we went, I tried to see through the eyes of Luke, a newcomer to the area. I saw things I'd never noticed before. Like restaurants that really didn't have the best coffee in town, in spite of their placemat advertising. And streets that had been neglected, sadly, by an underfunded road commission.

For a while, I apologized to Luke every time he hit a pothole in the road, but it grew tiresome. "You'll just have to remember where they are, like the rest of us," I said.

I cringed as we drove past the closed and boarded-up storefronts—a result of the recession. I was truly sad for the ruined dreams and livelihoods the CLOSED signs represented. There were foreclosed homes in town too, and more than a few with perpetual yard sales in their driveway, as residents tried to earn their next mortgage payment or grocery run.

In turn, Luke was a great resource for me, as I'd agreed to teach for the first time since completing my degree some thirteen years ago. Walking into the classroom on day one was sheer terror. My legs felt like jelly and my heart was pounding. But each day got a little easier. In the evening I'd give Luke a recap—sharing the highs and the lows.

"Just be yourself, Kaker Mayne," Luke would say every night, with great confidence.

Somehow, this amazing man felt that everyone in the world would love me as much as he did, if I just let them get to know me.

I only wished that were true in the case of Bella and Wren. They seemed to have more important things to do than get to know their aunt. Such as looking at their phones, examining the tips of their hair for split ends, and gazing at their perfect toenails.

12

"Go jump in the lake" my wife said.
"Thank you I will" I said.
-KERBY LODGE GUEST BOOK-

"Here come the brides," I said into my phone, when Chip's number went to voicemail, yet again, "and they're getting rained on!"

Along with my construction team, landscapers were also hard to pin down in August. Like everyone else along the lake, they preferred to be out on their boats instead of taking down my grove of pine trees. And why not—winter will be here soon enough. Between November and March, it's the memories of these perfect summer days that keep us warm.

In my message, I asked Chip to just give me a rough timeframe of when he and his crew might arrive, and I reminded him of my mid-September deadline for staging a few wedding photos on the grounds of Kerby Lodge.

In return, Chip sent me a text with a yellow "thumbs up" icon and a smiley face.

"Hollis," I said, walking into the dining room, "will you be my bride?"

"Oh Kay," she said without turning around, "I'm actually seeing someone."

I smiled and explained that I needed to stage a photo shoot in early September, in order to turn Kerby Lodge into a hot spot for destination weddings.

"You're adorable, Hollis," I said, "every bride will hope to look just like you."

Hollis swiveled around in her chair and faced me squarely.

"A wedding destination is a big deal, Kay—it will change the DNA of this place," she said. "Are you prepared for that?"

"I'm prepared to be very successful," I said, a little defensively, "and there's already major interest—even without the tent. Brides love the rustic setting of Kerby Lodge."

"Brides are trouble." Hollis surprised me by saying.

"Are they?" I asked, genuinely intrigued.

"Yes," she said, "that's Hotel Management 101."

"Go on," I said.

"Brides just think they want a rustic setting," she explained, "but when it comes to the big day, what they expect is perfection. And creating that level of wedding perfection... here," Hollis went on to say while shaking her head, "will be next to impossible."

For such a cheery girl, she was a real downer on this topic.

Again, I thought of my own celebration... here. It was an epic family party; a true local celebration. More about people, and less about image, or pretense.

Luke and I had been married for several weeks, so there were no nerves, and no unmet expectations of the day, which just so happened to turn out beautifully.

And if there had been rain and lightning on my reception day? We would have laughed and run inside the lodge to pick up where we left off. That's because Kerby Lodge was my home. I knew every inch, and where the surplus buffet plates and linens were stored. We'd simply dry off with my stack of beach towels, set up the dining room, and carry on.

"...limo parking, an outdoor electrical system, bridal dressing rooms, floral refrigerators..."

I realized that as my mind was wandering to my own lovely party, Hollis was listing the additional resources Kerby Lodge would need to offer brides for their wedding day. Admittedly, many I hadn't thought of myself.

"Plus," she said, "brides will expect to meet with an event consultant when they come here—and that's not you, and it's not me."

Yikes, that's something I really hadn't thought of.

"With the added insurance and the costly maintenance," Hollis droned on, "I'm sure your uncle Zeke would agree that it's a risky investment."

Ugh, she played the Zeke card!

I never should have given her his number.

"Maybe Zeke would agree with you if he knew," I conceded, feeling like a child being schooled, "which he doesn't—yet."

Hollis raised her eyebrows at this.

"But I plan on moving forward," I stubbornly said, and left the room.

After all, I still owned the inn, didn't I? Wasn't my name on the brochure? Not for the first time since returning home, I felt out of place in my own lodge. I was a plastic totem pole—a big stuffed brown bear.

Have another cookie, Kay.

Go take a nap Kay, there's nothing you need to do here.

The air was hot and still, with barely a breeze. I woke up from my nap feeling too warm, and slightly sweaty. Still agitated from my earlier conversation, I would join the girls and cool off in the lake, I decided.

The girls had been spending their days on the beach with Max and a few other summer kids. Each time I poked my head out the door, they were laughing too loud and splashing too much. Thankfully, they preferred to be down the beach from the other guests and their small children, who might feel intimidated by all the exuberance.

Or maybe that was just a ghost from my own childhood. As I walked down the path and towards the rambunctious teens, old insecurities came flooding back.

Look at all those kids Kaker—go make friends!

How many times had I heard that growing up? It was so easy for Mum and Dad to be friendly with everyone who visited the lodge, and indeed they made some genuine friendships over the years. They stayed in touch through Christmas cards and letters. Our family was often invited to the graduations and weddings of our returning guests—some of whom the Kerby family had known for twenty and thirty years.

But unlike Raya, I could not make a friend in a week's time. It was not in my nature. It would take me most of the week to screw up the nerve to join in their play, and by then they'd be getting ready to leave. With a new group of kids on their heels.

These teens on the beach today were no different from the kids I steered clear of every summer of my life—only now, I owned this stretch of shoreline, and two of those teens were family. Yet I felt unexpectedly bashful. So much so that while still hidden behind a cover of pines, I turned back towards the lodge.

Across the parking pad, I saw Jennifer talking to a customer and considered visiting with her. Not long ago, I would have done this without thinking, but that was before Europe. Before I had gotten salty with Jennifer for not calling me.

She looked up and caught my eye, then coolly turned away.

Great.

Rebuffed, I pivoted and went back inside the lodge, giving my intern—my not-so-trusty sidekick—a wide berth.

I was now avoiding Bella and Wren, in addition to Hollis.

I was avoiding Jennifer, my best friend since high school, who was also avoiding me.

I was avoiding Zeke and June, who I hadn't told about my wedding venue plans.

Jack and Stace were off enjoying the last days of summer, along with every contractor who might otherwise be finishing my lodge repairs. I hadn't seen Daniel since we returned from our trip, and Luke was at his conferences.

Marj Maki and her sign-up sheet was looking pretty good right about now.

"You should feel like an outsider with Bella and Wren, Kaker," Luke was now saying on the phone. It was evening, and I caught him with a few free minutes. "You're an outsider. A woman, in the company of kids. That's how every parent of every teenager feels—trust me."

"I trust you, Luke. I know you're right," I whined, "but I wanted things to be different. I wanted the girls to like me, and hang out with me."

"Kay," he said with an impatience in his voice I was not used to hearing, "you spent twelve years hibernating in the lodge after your parents passed away. That was the bulk of Bella and Wren's young lives."

"Insightful," I said with an edge in my own voice, "but not helpful."

"You are strangers," he continued, though I thought I'd heard enough. Luke's was a lecture I was ready to walk out on.

Under his blunt tone, Luke was genuinely concerned, I could tell. "You see them as good kids, I just see them as kids," he went on, "and I'm a little worried, Kay. A lot can go wrong."

This was too much. I expected encouragement, not this brain dump of advice, shoe-horned in between his precious conference speakers.

I tried not to tune out as Luke talked. But it was *blah blah blah* structure, and *blah blah blah* guidance. He thought they were going to take advantage of my inexperience, and my desire for their approval.

I was adamant that would not happen, and that Bella and Wren just needed a little time to settle in. After a few more days of rest, I told him, I would be feeling like my old self again, and would get the girls involved in some fun activities with me.

47

"It's… just…" I attempted to put words to my feelings, but felt constricted by the time. I was sure Luke was watching the clock, and would need to go soon.

I was trying to tell him that I feared Tad and Selby would never let the girls come to Kerby Lodge again if I didn't get this right. Then Tad wouldn't come back again, ever. But my mind wandered until I realized Luke was saying something about Hollis.

"Sorry," I said, "what was that again?"

"I said, please keep Hollis on for the rest of the summer, so you don't have to think about Kerby Lodge." I bristled at his comment, and the innuendo that I was less than capable.

"My mother managed to run the lodge with a couple of teenagers," I said.

"But you're not Raya," Luke said, rather sharply I thought.

Ouch.

"And you're not Fitz," I shot back.

So, how about those crockpots?

13

"Wait. You want us to *work*?" Bella was asking me the next day while we ate a late dinner in the apartment.

"I wouldn't call it working," I said. "Let's say contributing."

"But we're your guests," Wren chimed in.

"A month is a long time to be a guest," I said, "and you're both Kerby's at Kerby Lodge. That means something—to me it does. It used to mean something to your dad, too."

"Free labor," Bella said.

Growing up, I often thought Tad's quiet secret was that he actually enjoyed our year-round life at the lodge—much more than I did. What I came to realize was that Tad enjoyed life itself, no matter where he was. But he had bigger dreams than Kerby Lodge could hold.

My brother told me once that 18 years of rustic living on Lake Michigan was plenty for him. Now, he and his wife and daughters preferred vast oceans, and the salt-water swimming pools of all-inclusive resorts.

Tad wasn't ungenerous. Early in his career, he regularly invited me and our parents to visit, or to join his young family on vacations. I was often busy with school, but our parents accepted while still healthy enough to travel.

Fitz and Raya longed to spend time with their granddaughters. They regretted, though never to Tad's face, that the girls could never spare any summer days to visit them at the lodge.

Privately, it broke their hearts that their granddaughters would never get to experience what they thought of as the best life had to offer: a Lake Michigan summer at Kerby Lodge—their grandchildren's namesake.

But not, as it turned out, their inheritance.

While I inherited the whole of Kerby Lodge and its acreage, Tad inherited a valuable piece of undeveloped land on an exclusive inland lake nearby. For a hot minute, I dreamed of Tad and Selby building a vacation home there, and being my summer neighbors. But he sold the land immediately, and purchased a second home in Savannah, Georgia. Closer to his home.

It made sense on paper, but not to my heart.

Still, there was no denying that Tad and I had a loving and happy childhood. We were stronger for being part of a family at our family-run business. I would stick to my guns.

"I'm not asking you to cut down trees and build a cabin—but I do want you to find a way to be useful each day," I said. "You can ask Hollis or Jennifer for suggestions. Or come to me."

Bella rolled her eyes, and Wren pursed her lips.

"Fine," Bella said, clearing her dishes. "We'd better get some rest, lil' sister. The most horrible vacation in the world is about to take a nose dive."

"I reckon," Wren said, and then mouthed the words *good night* before heading into the bunk room and closing the door.

Horrible vacation? Horrible, horrible girl, I was tempted to say. Instead, I angrily grabbed a cookie and my mug of tea, and made my way to the great room to catch the last of the sunset sky, and enjoy a few moments of peace.

Taking a sip, I closed my eyes and leaned my head back. Were there really just a few weeks left of summer? And would every day between now and Labor Day be this painful? I remember when our lodge was all about having the Kerby family on the premises—the more the merrier.

The best sign that summer was near was the return of Aunt June and Uncle Zeke from their winter home in Florida. After visiting with Gram for an hour or so, and moving their suitcases into her guestroom in the house up the hill, they would appear with their sweatshirts and work gloves to "report for duty."

We'd refer to the long lists Fitz and Raya had written on worn yellow legal pads. Surfaces would need to be washed. A great many sheets needed to be pulled out of mothballs and laundered. Every cupboard needed a complete spring cleaning as it was just assumed that mice and spiders had passed their winters among the dishes, mugs, and pots and pans.

"Dunna be squeamish lass," Mum would say, as she flicked the intruders out the door with the business end of her dish towel.

Doors and windows were thrown open.

Rugs were dragged out and supported by any fence post or lawn chair that would hold them while Tad beat the dust out of them with a tennis racket.

The sun would be higher and warmer, melting the mounds of snow and turning them into streams of water running over rocks and around trees as it rushed back to the big lake.

We'd end each day on the bluff overlooking the lakeshore as the sun went down, laughing and talking while Dad grilled our dinner—hard-earned bottles of cold cream soda in everyone's hand.

The warmth dropped off quickly as the sun set. And we'd tramp into the warm apartment kitchen, to feast on burgers, chicken, potato salad, baked beans and chocolate cake.

It was never the hard work I rebelled from, I realized. It was the lodge itself, and the way Mum and Dad would be distracted during peak season. While I loved all the shoulder season traditions, the gatherings and the cookouts, none had stood the test of time.

So all the fun things fell away, leaving me with an imbalanced life.

All the drudgery, with none of the chocolate cake.

"A cookout!" I said out loud as this epiphany popped into my head.

Labor Day weekend was perfect—Luke would be home. Tad and Selby and the girls would be here. I'd invite Daniel, along with Nan and Sperry. Hopefully, Zeke and June could come up from Florida. And of course, Jack and Stace, and Hollis.

Jennifer and Patrick might come—if they're talking to me by then.

The girls would be less than enthused. I could practically hear them say they don't eat *this* and they don't eat *that*. *Cook outside with the bugs and bats? Eww!*

The girls are spoiled, certainly, and Selby is to blame. Tad and I were never indulged the way Bella and Wren are. They want to play and be entertained. If our cell reception wasn't so spotty at the lodge, I'd never even get a chance to talk with the girls.

But I wouldn't let anyone dampen my enthusiasm over what would surely be a memorable gathering. The first of many to come.

I'm not sure when I fell asleep on the great room sofa, but I fought to wake up enough to go to bed. Before standing, I checked my own phone, and saw that Luke had called and it had gone right to my voicemail.

My hands shook as I pressed the button to listen.

"Kaker, sweetheart, I'm so sorry for being bullish earlier," he said.

I let go of the tension in my neck as I listened to Luke's voice.

"Of course you're more than capable. Having Hollis stay just gives you time to spend with the girls—that's all I was thinking. Let them get to know you, because when they do, they will have to conclude that you are amazing."

I smiled as I listened to Luke.

"Do whatever it takes to get close to the girls," he went on. "Take some money out of the bank and go to Petoskey for a few days. Go shopping!"

"Buy their love," he said.

14

Decks and Docks. Flips and Flops.
That's what Kerby Lodge summers are made of.
-KERBY LODGE GUEST BOOK-

Could I buy the girls' love?

Not many knew that I had enough money to take a serious stab at it.

I didn't realize I'd married into money until a month after our courthouse wedding. That's when I discovered that the little mom-and-pop jewelry store I thought Nan and Sperry Mayne owned was in fact Mayne Fine Jewelers, with nine locations throughout Chicagoland.

They didn't just live in an apartment, they lived in the *penthouse* apartment of the Mayne building. Had I done any research at all on my laptop, I would have found Nan and Sperry's names all over the society pages, and associated with several charities.

Photos of Nan—at fundraising balls and the NICU ward of the children's hospital—revealed a tall beauty with the slender physique of an avid golfer. Her kind eyes were Luke's, and her dark curls were Daniel's.

By her side in every picture was the handsome Sperry, with his charming smile and graying temples. If I had wanted to know what both Daniel and Luke would look like in another 25 years, Sperry was all the proof I needed.

But I didn't even think to look.

I was too busy making assumptions, and living in the moment, and running around the grounds of the lodge with my poor-as-a-church-mouse fiancée, Luke.

Showing off my *Hey Hey, We're The Monkees* beach towel.

Two days before our reception, I watched the Mayne's drive down the lodge road in a three-vehicle caravan, and my first thought was, "the circus is coming to town."

Nan and Sperry, the ringmasters, took the lead in their Land Rover.

Following close behind was a brand new 4-wheel drive SUV in a champagne finish with leather interiors. It still had the dealer sticker on the window. Behind that was a shiny new truck filled with, I quickly found out, Ethan Allen furniture.

Luke introduced his parents. It was more formal than it ought to have been because in turn, they quickly introduced Jeb and John—the young, hunky drivers of the truck and SUV.

Luke helped Jeb and John unpack Nan's "gently used" Ethan Allen sunroom furniture into our storage garage, as if this kind of grand entrance was an everyday occurrence. Nan said, "I thought these pieces might be charming in the A-Frame, when the twins tackle that space."

I could only nod in my dazed state.

Nan had been an ardent follower of Daniel's *ReMayne* blog. She had tracked and commented on every space we renovated, and talked about young brother-sister decorators Jack and Stace Wildberry, the twins, as if they were family members.

My head was spinning as I simultaneously met my in-laws for the first time, wrapped my head around the furniture they brought, and wondered who the SUV belonged to.

And Jeb and John—were they staying for the party? If so, would I seat them with Nan and Sperry, or at the kid's table? But as quickly as they had arrived, the two men shook everyone's hand, got in the truck and drove back up the hill.

"Thank you for the lovely wedding gift," I said, collecting myself and gazing at the shrink-wrapped wood and rattan set, covered in luscious Teal and Aspen basket-weave textiles.

"Kakah," Nan laughed in her broad Boston accent, as her hand fluttered casually in the air. "This is just a few castoffs among family." Later, Jack and Stace drooled over the quality of the pieces, though the A-Frame had been way down on our renovation list at the time.

"What's this SUV?" Luke was asking his parents. "Are you traveling with a spare?"

"For you two!" Nan said. "A little belated engagement gift." She held her hand up to deflect any pushback and said, "You'll thank us with the first snow."

I was speechless. The SUV likely cost more than I would make in a year at the school.

But the real kicker was their actual gift. Nan and Sperry wrote a check that made me choke on the cake I was eating when we opened the card. After Luke brought me a sip of water, I looked at him like there must be some mistake. He smiled and shrugged.

"We'll throw it in the bank for now," he said. "Could come in handy."

Handy?

"Like, if we wanted to donate a wing to the hospital?" I asked.

"It's just money Kaker," Luke said laughing, reading my shocked face.

"I thought everything you owned was in a duffel bag," I said, eyes wide.

"That's true," Luke said. "And because that's true, I have a healthy savings."

That made sense.

"And… a trust fund," he said, a little sheepishly.

"But neither of us have ever been motivated by money—not a day in our lives," he pointed out. "So my parents' wealth was never worth mentioning."

I nodded.

"And thank you for marrying this poor teacher," Luke said, smiling. Referring to himself in the self-deprecating way I'd come to love—especially given that he had no idea how charming and handsome he was. I swear, if he didn't shave every morning, he'd probably never even look in the mirror.

"But why did you marry me?" I asked, smiling back.

"I married you because…" and here Luke stopped and stared into my eyes.

"Because?" I nudged. "My collection of flannel shirts? My wildlife eviction skills?"

"Because, beautiful girl," he said, taking both of my hands in his own, "you have the heart of a teacher and the face of an angel. And you needed me—as much as I needed you."

My eyes fluttered on an unexpected tear.

15

Sum Summers
are Better 'n Nuthers.
-KERBY LODGE GUEST BOOK-

"There's no free lunch, Kaker."

Uncle Zeke supported my theory that I would have several surprise expenses, even if most of the renovations at the A-Frame and Gram's house were covered by insurance.

"Sure, they will pay for some, but not all. And higher rates are lurking... you better believe it," he said.

Zeke and June had retired from their accounting business, but still played an important role as my financial advisors. And often, my duel life coaches.

"Have you talked to Daniel yet?" June asked, taking the phone from Zeke.

"No. I haven't seen him since we've been back," I said.

"It's not going to get any easier, Kaker," she said.

And she was right.

Zeke and June both agreed with me that with the renovations on the A-Frame, it would make sense to rent it out, instead of letting Daniel stay for a day or two here and there, whenever he was in town. But I hated to take the A-Frame away from him when he had been the reason Kerby Lodge was profitable again.

My stomach hurt thinking about that conversation, and about the other ways that this last gasp of summer was ruining my life.

56

I was definitely not any closer to the girls. And no closer to fulfilling my destination wedding dreams, which I was too cowardly to share with Zeke and June. And I couldn't seem to nail down a date with Chip to remove the pine grove.

He and I were playing a very lackluster game of phone tag.

16

You're doing a fine job with the lodge, Kay.
We loved your parents, but wish you well.
-KERBY LODGE GUEST BOOK-

Gram died before Wren was born.

And Wren was just a wee babe when Raya, her grandmother, died. The poor young girl had no concept of all she had missed by not having these two lovely women in her life, as I had.

Bella was hardly any luckier, though she may have a few hazy memories of Raya. What really saddened me was that neither girl had any sense of curiosity about their grandmother, or their great-grandmother.

Or me, for that matter.

Nevertheless, a week into their stay I invited Bella and Wren to ride up the road with me in the golf cart to see Gram's house. I wanted to go and inspect the progress, slow though it was. I thought they might be interested in going too, and talking about Gram.

Only Wren took me up on my offer, but I soon found out it was because she discovered the strong cell reception by the main road. Specifically, near the old fenced-in tennis courts. I was surprised when Wren hopped off, and gave me a little *toodles* wave of her fingers before jogging over to the old wooden bench. Rather than come in Gram's house with me.

I exhaled my disapproval, which Wren either didn't hear, or ignored.

Bella had wanted to stay behind at the lodge, to catch up on her assigned summer reading for an AP literature class, she said. She had a few more books to annotate—including *Lord of the Flies*, which sat on the table this morning at breakfast.

"Now, that's a book you never forget," I said, buttering my toast.

And for a moment, over coffee, I allowed myself to daydream about a *Lord of the Flies* scenario, with Kerby Lodge as the desert island. I pictured myself stranded here with Bella, Wren, and Hollis. And, just for kicks, Uncle Zeke.

No doubt, Zeke and Hollis would form an alliance to overrule my wedding tent. Bella would turn the others against me—telling them I wash towels during peak utility rates. And Wren would stay cool and collected, *sippin'* sweet tea until we were rescued.

As I climbed the steps onto Gram's deck, a small orange car sped down the lodge road. We were expecting new guests today, but I also wondered if it was Max's car, the one I'd been hearing about. The little FIAT that his parents gave him to "have a little fun with" during his senior year of high school.

Gram's house had moved forward, incrementally. Some of the repairs had been made, just as they had in the A-Frame. When they got to the cosmetics—the paint on the walls, and the bamboo flooring—the rest would go quickly.

If the flooring was in, I could do the rest. After spending an entire winter and spring renovating every room and hallway in the lodge, as well as a handful of cabins, this girl knew how to paint. My arms ached, just thinking about all that Daniel and I achieved on our own.

Looking at the silent empty spaces now, I thought of Gram's old furniture, stored in the dry garage for safe keeping, next to Nan's Ethan Allen sunroom set that hadn't moved in a year.

A short month ago I was ready to toss all of the highly unusual pieces.

I always knew that Gram Kerby had a style that was different from the rustic furnishings found in the great room and lodge. No oversized pieces for Gram, her sofas and chairs were square, squat and boxy. In contrast to the big log coffee table in the lodge, Gram's was small, with an irregular geometric shape.

"It can all go," I told the decorating twins before leaving for Europe, gesturing to the "mod" furnishings as we did a walk-through of Gram's house—my house. The *Mayne* house.

"Are you sure?" Stace asked, looking slightly alarmed.

"Quite sure," I said, gesturing to the metallic 70s wallpaper in the living room, in shades of orange, brown and dark green. "I don't see Luke and I hosting fondue parties, or taking macramé classes, do you?"

I wanted a current look, and told Jack and Stace just that.

"If the charity store doesn't want it, then I guess we can toss it all on a bonfire," I said.

Jack nearly choked when I said this last comment, and reached for something to hold onto while his knees buckled. His sister had to bring him his eco-friendly water bottle so he could catch his breath. Jack loosened the Windsor knot on his tie, and took a swig.

"Sit down for a minute Kay," Stace said, "there's something you need to see."

Pulling up an orange kidney-shaped ottoman, I did as she asked.

Minutes later, Jack and Stace were opening images on their computer and showing me the current value of the Herman Miller Eames chair resting in the corner, and Gram's Danish teak sideboard from Haywood-Wakefield.

I couldn't believe my eyes.

And Gram's "goofy plastic dining chairs," as I had once referred to them, are original Saarinen Tulip Chairs, as it turns out—worth a small fortune.

"The sofa is a vintage *Drexel*," Stace said, in breathy reverence.

Looking at the numbers, I just about did a spit take. I had no idea how valuable these pieces were—this furniture that Tad and I plopped on in sandy bathing suits as kids, and curled up on with dripping mugs of hot cocoa during blizzards. Now perfectly preserved in this under-utilized home.

"Why Gram Kerby," I said, smiling, "you clever little Mid-Century minx."

Her leather and stainless steel sling chairs were in perfect condition, the Wildberry's told me. The sofa could use new upholstery, as could the Danish Baumritter side chairs, but otherwise Gram's furniture just needed fresh surroundings to show them off. We all agreed that everything was getting lost against the "hippy" wallcoverings.

Thankfully, no one argued to keep the green shag carpets!

Armed with new information, I decided to keep Gram's furniture. With a few like-new pieces from Wildberry Consignment Shop, the house would take on a fresh modern look. "Perfect for the town's new power couple," Jack had said, with a smile.

"Power *outage* couple you mean," I said, thinking how many times we had to run the backup generator at Gram's house during this past harsh winter.

Walking back to the lodge, I hoped that Bella and Wren had found some way to occupy their day. I didn't see either girl anywhere.

While I was up the road, Hollis had checked a family in—the Grays—who would be staying in a cabin for two weeks. Stuart and Joy Gray were young, and had a small boy of four named Cody. When I entered the great room, they were exploring the books and games.

Little Cody Gray was excited to see the lake and pulled at his dad's shirt to go swimming. The dad wasn't as enthused, and gently swatted Cody away, giving a sidelong glance to his wife that made me cringe. Most families couldn't wait to go swimming in Lake Michigan, and the weather today was perfect.

He told the boy to go down there by himself, and they'd catch up with him later.

I froze.

"Uh… we don't have a lifeguard," I tried to keep the terror out of my voice as I injected myself into their conversation. "Young children need to be with an adult at the beach," I said, bluntly. "The currents are strong."

As Stuart Gray frowned and reluctantly nodded, I could hear another car quietly pulling up in the parking lot outside the lodge.

Who now?

17

Now I have to go back to my real life.
But for one glorious week, I was queen of the pontoon boat.
-KERBY LODGE GUEST BOOK-

"Kaker!"

A great cloud of dark curls with an equally somber demeanor came striding into the great room minutes later, in the form of Daniel Mayne. I never knew when he'd drop in.

We greeted each other with a hug.

Tanned and handsome, his face looked unusually strained as he nodded to Hollis.

"My production got delayed," he told me, "so I came home to enjoy the lake instead of sitting in my hotel room."

Home!

I enjoyed hearing Daniel refer to Kerby Lodge as home.

He would always have a place here.

If it weren't for Daniel Mayne, I could very well be out of a home myself. I came very close to losing everything to a shortage of guests and unpaid taxes. If he hadn't helped me revive the lodge and several of the cabins, I don't think I could have attracted enough visitors to keep it running.

That's why it grieved me to tell him the A-Frame couldn't be his drop-in home for much longer—it was just an economic reality. With the forced renovations, triggered by the leak, the A-Frame could bring in a hefty rental fee. And the second peak season, the fall color season, was quickly approaching.

I could have Hollis put the A-Frame on VeRoom.com, and we would have it fully booked in no time—through early November.

When I thought about talking to Daniel, I felt disloyal to the man. But Aunt June was right, it wouldn't get any easier.

"You know the living area of the A-Frame is still unfinished, right?" I asked.

"That's okay," he said. "I can sleep upstairs, and spend time on the deck or beach."

I nodded.

I was sure the girls would want to see him, but I had lost track of them. They'd turn up though. I almost asked where his girlfriend Francine was these days, but stopped myself. I didn't want to be the only one bringing her up. Daniel certainly didn't mention her. I tried to remember when I saw her last. It had been several months.

As I was about to invite him to join me for an iced tea, Daniel interrupted.

"Let's go outside Kaker, and take a short walk. There's something I want you to see." From the serious look on his face, I suspected it might not be a stroll in the park.

A heavy feeling settled in my already precarious stomach as I followed Daniel. As we walked between the pines and silently approached the A-Frame, Daniel motioned for me to be as quiet as possible.

Whatever we were going to find was something Daniel didn't want to startle. Raccoons? Bear cubs? I only wished it were wild animals—I knew how to deal with those. Instead, my heart sank as I realized it was far, far worse.

Teenagers.

From the side of the A-Frame that faced the water, I could hear murmurs and talking coming from the deck—hidden away from the path. Bursts of laughter were drowning out our quiet footsteps. And the words became clearer as we got closer.

"So where's your uncle—the one who stays in this cabin?" Was that Max's voice?

My mouth fell open in true surprise, but I remained silent as I looked up at Daniel.

"Uncle Daniel is away for a few more days," I could hear Bella saying— a little too loudly for someone who was trying to hide.

"Ahh, so we're all alone." Max's voice answered Bella.

Laughter followed, along with other sounds such as glass on glass, and paper crinkling.

Daniel's arm was suddenly in front of my waist, gently but firmly holding me back from running to the deck, to confront Max and Bella.

"You're so pretty Bella," Max was saying.

Bella responded by giggling—I could hear that she was trying to stop, but was having trouble. Her voice sounded muffled. Was she tipsy? Were they kissing?

"So... can we get inside Uncle Daniel's cabin, do you think?" Max was asking.

"Umm..." she was deliberating her answer.

By now Bella knew where the master keys were, and for all I knew, she had one with her. She was at the point of making a monumental life decision.

Daniel made it for her.

"No you can't." Daniel spoke to both Max and Bella as we came around the corner to face them both, as they sat on the deck. Bella startled and stood up quickly, while Max remained sitting, smirking at us.

Between them sat a nearly empty bottle of Chateau de Mi chardonnay, with a sticky note on the label that read Room 5. There was also a block of cheese and a box of crackers with sticky notes that read Room 3. These two had raided the wine cooler—my guest refrigerator.

It must have been while Hollis was giving the Gray family a tour.

I didn't know where to aim my anger.

"Uncle Daniel, you're back," Bella was saying. "Aunt Kay, we were just talking, honest."

"Honest?" I said. "You stole from my guests, and you're drinking right under my nose! There's no honesty going on here Bella."

"Relax everybody," Max was slurring to Daniel and I, as if we were children having tantrums. "It's just a cheap bottle of wine. I'll leave a twenty on the table before I go and..."

Max didn't get a chance to finish his sentence. Daniel had picked him up by the popped collar of his Oxford shirt, and was fast-walking him to his BMW by holding tightly to his upper arm. He stuffed Max into the passenger seat, and before Max could react, Daniel drove up the hill and onto the main road. Presumably to take him home.

The look on Max's face was nearly better than any forced apology I would ever get from the boy, who would have to come back to Kerby Lodge when he was sober to drive his little FIAT home again.

After watching the BMW drive up the lodge road, Bella and I turned to look at each other. We both had the same stunned expression at how quickly Daniel had acted. Finally, we rallied to register the underlying anger each of us felt towards the other.

Bella turned to storm back to the lodge, while I bent down to clean up the mess she and Max had left on the deck.

"Typical," I said under my breath, and jogged to catch up with her.

18

"You're not my mom!" Bella declared, shouting as she stomped her way back to the lodge, "you're not my dad!"

"I know, I know," I said, trying to keep up with her. A few guests from the cabins stuck their heads out of their screen doors to see what the commotion was.

How was it that my niece had turned the tables on this conversation so quickly, and put me on the defensive? Why was I trying to calm her down instead of the other way around?

Is this what teenagers did?

I struggled to keep up with the fast walking Bella, as a sharp cramp developed in the side of my rib cage—a *stitch*, as Raya would have called it. I wished Luke were here. Though I knew that this was my dilemma to solve.

Besides, all I could hear in my head was Luke's dire warnings about teenagers. How they would take advantage of my lack of experience, and push my buttons. I'm sure Luke would criticize me for not setting boundaries and rules for Bella.

How had I allowed Max to show up here, anyway—without any supervision? What would have happened if Daniel had not discovered their little party of two?

Bella herself interrupted my thoughts, and thankfully stopped walking so that I could stop too. My ribs were aching.

"Stop following me! I do not need you—I never have!" She turned so she could yell at me. I could see angry tears rolling down her face. I wondered how many sips of the wine she had with Max, and how much of her righteous indignation was the alcohol talking.

Surely she could not have a lot of experience with drinking at her age, with the ever watchful Tad and Selby as parents.

I looked at this young girl, realizing what a stranger she was to me. I hardly knew her—though because I could see so much of her father, and my father, in her face, I desperately loved her. At that moment, I wanted nothing more than to bridge the gap between us.

"Can we just be friends Bella?" I implored, nearly in tears myself.

"I. Have. Friends," she declared.

"Lots of friends," Bella said, crying angrily. "Friends I had plans with this summer. Friends I wanted to be with. I'm going into my senior year! And I'm missing so much. *So much.* I'm missing dances and parties, and shopping trips and dates. By the time I get home from this backwater town, I'll be on the outside of everything, and everyone."

And then she levelled her cruelest blow.

"Here's a postcard for you *Kaker*," she hissed. *"Having a crap time at Kerby Lodge!"*

My head jerked back as if I'd been slapped—and then it hit me. Bella and Wren did not want to be here, as Tad said they did. My initial instincts were right that this wasn't how they wanted to spend their summer. It was... inflicted on them.

Kerby Lodge was their punishment, I realized, astonished. And I was their jailer.

Of course.

Tad and Selby wanted this, not my nieces.

The girls could have called me any time if they'd wanted to visit, but they never had. Why this summer? After taking a few deep breaths, I paused to allow the tightness in the surrounding air to be released. Finally, I broke the ice.

"Okay Bella," I said quietly. "I had no idea that you were here under duress, and I'm sorry. Of course you'd want to be at home this summer. Senior year is a big deal."

She was simmering down a bit, I could tell. So I ventured another try.

"I love you, and I only want to be your aunt," I said.

But Bella was not ready for an olive branch.

"You should have thought of that years ago. You hardly ever came to see us—we were just a Christmas card and a birthday card to you," she said with amazing control in her voice.

"You look at Wren and me as the sweet faces that grew up a little each year, but you have no idea who we are."

At that truth, my tears did fall. And I was helpless to stop them.

She was right.

"Bella is hurting, Kay. She's self-medicating," Luke said over the phone.

After the girls were in their room, with Wren murmuring to Bella in an indistinguishable, but consoling voice, I wandered up to the bench by the tennis courts and called Luke. More than good cell reception, I wanted to be out of earshot.

"Self-medicating—with wine?" I was alarmed at the thought and implications.

"Not likely. I'd say she's looking for attention—from Max, other kids in town, maybe from you," he said. "Look, Bella wants what she wants. She had a vision of what her senior summer would be like, and her parents, for whatever reason, took her toys away."

"Then why isn't she mad at them?" I asked.

He laughed a little. "She is mad at them, but they aren't here," he said, "you are."

Luke was right, Bella needed boundaries, and she needed my love and support. But I had no idea how to begin, especially when she wanted nothing to do with me.

Would we all survive the rest of August?

19

Like a bad penny, Max showed up again the next day—but he wasn't alone.

Looking out the window from the kitchen late the next morning, I watched a shiny Lexus pull into the circle drive and park. Max got out of the passenger side and surveyed the grounds.

He was nervous, I thought. Perhaps he was waiting for Daniel to ambush him.

I smiled a little at the memory of Max's shocked face.

Next, a stocky woman unfolded herself from the driver's seat, wearing a lime green golf skirt and pink oxford shirt with the collar standing up. Her silver hair was fashionably short, and her skin had an all-over tan that was a result of a privileged summer lifestyle of boating, golf and tennis. I'd seen that smooth, even tan many times in my years on Lake Michigan, and could spot it a mile away.

She took her sunglasses off to appraise my property, and her nose wrinkled slightly. She had the same look on her face that Bella did last week, in town.

Something smelled unsavory to this woman, and for my money, it was Kerby Lodge.

"Lilian Atwater," she said as she came at me in the great room, hand outstretched. When we shook, her gold bracelets jangled on her freckled wrist.

"Kay Kerby Mayne," I said. "I'm the owner."

Lilian nodded.

"I believe our young people are friends. My Max seems to have forgotten something here," she said. Max, I saw, had moved into the dining room, and was talking to Hollis. No doubt he was avoiding me, which didn't speak well for his character.

He was letting mommy do his dirty work.

"You know boys," Lilian continued, "always leaving their things strewn about."

Strewn?

As if he'd left a sock in my driveway, and not a sports car.

"I don't have children, Lilian," I said. "But I do know that people of all ages will leave things strewn about if we keep cleaning up their messes."

Lilian's eyes narrowed, and her mouth opened to respond. But just then, Bella and Wren came into the room wearing pretty sun dresses, looking as though they were ready to host a group of debutantes in the parlor.

"You must be Mrs. Atwater," Bella said, approaching Lilian, and avoiding eye contact with me. "I'm Bella Kerby and this is Wren," she crooned. "Can we offer you coffee?"

Bella glanced sideways at me as she spoke, silently accusing me of having the abhorrent manners of a northerner.

"Bella, darling," Lilian stammered, "you are as pretty as Max said. Thank you, no. I won't keep you, I'm sure Max is anxious to say hello." Lilian gestured expansively towards the dining room, as if she were the *grand dame* of my own home.

The girls nodded and wandered away. Lilian and I renewed our eye contact as the young people talked and laughed. Lilian broke away first, and let her gaze travel around the room.

"My my, just look at how you've gussied the place up," she said, as if it were a little princess fort instead of a renovated lodge. "I haven't been here in years—not since we had a large number of guests one summer, and I was vetting a nice place for them to sleep."

"Oh?" I said, "did they enjoy their stay?"

"They did," she said, "at the Redbird Inn, up the road."

It took every muscle in my face to not react.

"Did you say your name was Mayne now?" Lilian was walking around my room like a peacock in full feather—knowing that she had ruffled me. She was looking at my furniture and artwork. Her eyes widened as they landed on my wedding ring.

Her next question was softer, and made me wonder if she hadn't felt she'd gone too far.

"Any relation to Mayne Fine Jewelers in Chicago?" she asked, "Skip and I make a jaunt there every December for a new little bauble or two. Nan Mayne always takes the time to welcome us, and to personally show us her latest inventory."

She had me.

I couldn't outright lie, but I certainly did not want to play the "who do we both know" game with Lilian Atwater and impress her through my in-laws. But I didn't want to insult Lilian, who was obviously a client of Nan and Sperry—maybe even a friend of theirs.

This was new territory for me.

In many ways, it was much easier to be poor and on the verge of bankruptcy than to suddenly be among the wealthy without knowing the rules of conduct.

There should be a playbook.

I opened my mouth to confess that I was indeed related to these wonderful, successful people, but I was saved by the teens coming into the room in a swirl of laughter.

"Mother," Max said, "I'd like to whisk these lovelies to the yacht club for lunch. That is, if that's okay with you, Mrs. Mayne," he said deferentially, turning to nod at me as if our last exchange wasn't contentious.

I opened my mouth to object, but didn't get the chance.

"Of course! Young people should go do young things while the sun is shining," Lilian said expansively, "before they get old and leathery like us, right Kay?"

I closed my mouth and glanced over at Bella and Wren. One held my gaze in a defiant stare, daring me to ruin yet another day for her. The other sweetly fished around her pockets for lip gloss. *Bless you, sweet Wren.*

Every instinct told me to take control and keep the girls home, but as I scrambled to find justification for it, the situation seemed to be pried from my hands.

"Don't watch the clock Auntie Kay," Bella said, "Max might take us sailing after lunch if the breeze picks up." The girls left to go gather their beach bags but Lilian stopped Max.

"First, we have unfinished business Maxie," she said. She tried to make a show of offering me money to replace the wine the "children had accidentally" gotten into.

I waved it away.

"I can afford a bottle of wine, Lilian," I said. "The point is, Max and Bella took things that were not theirs to take. I want to impress upon them that it costs more to regain a guest's trust than it costs to buy a bottle of wine or box of crackers. Surely you can see that."

71

Not to mention, they were drinking, I wanted to yell.

Lilian tucked her money away, and smiled. "I'm sure that Max is used to our own little cottage, where everything is open for the hospitality of our guests."

Really? At age 17, little Maxie doesn't know that not everything belongs to him?

I was actually at a loss for words.

Just then, my unlikely hero was not Daniel, or even Luke, but a young and wise beyond her years Hollis Fanning—who walked in from the dining room to save the day.

"Max," Hollis said as she entered, "in case you get confused in the future, there's pop and juice boxes chilling out in the angler's ice chest. I keep them there for the younger guests."

Before Max could find the words to go with the indignation on his face, Hollis spoke again. "Oh and Kay," she said, making sure she had Lilian's and my full attention, "there are important influencers who want to know more about your Mid-Century Modern renovation. It's causing quite a stir in the design community."

I nodded without knowing what to say.

"I scheduled a meeting for you with your publicist this afternoon." And at that, Hollis turned on her heels and left the great room—leaving Max speechless, and Lilian gazing at me with a grudging respect.

"If you'll excuse me," I nodded at Lilian, "the influencers wait for no one."

20

Lilian's stressful visit drove me to the lake.

I hadn't been swimming since our trip, and desperately needed the lake's restorative waves and swells to knock the last of the jetlag out of my bones. Floating in Lake Michigan was nearly as good as a total body massage—although I'd rank the hot stones massage in the shadow of the Swiss Alps a close second.

The path to the lake is covered in soft pine needles, releasing a fresh balsam scent with every step of my bare feet. I could feel my blood pressure stabilizing as I passed under the tall pines and shadowy oaks. Towards the gentle splashes upon the shore.

Without hesitating, I tossed my beach towel over a fallen log, and stepped into the crystal clear water. The packed sand supported my feet as I took step after step, going deeper and deeper.

After the first cool shock, my body adjusted to the temperature of the fresh water, until it felt as though I were swimming in a sea of the softest, warmest silk. Leaning back, I floated effortlessly with my arms outstretched—allowing the swells of the water to roll me back and forth. Pulling my tense muscles this way and that.

It was impossible to hang onto any stress, and I found myself exhaling and inhaling deeply. With my ears under water, there was only blessed silence. I closed my eyes for a moment, but preferred gazing upward as the water pushed and pulled, stretching me.

Many years ago, my dad taught me the art of floating in Lake Michigan. "It takes a peaceful countenance, Kaker," he told me, "and you're a natural."

My on-the-go mum couldn't float for beans.

I was ridiculously pleased that while other kids spent hours and hours thrashing about in the water, splashing and swimming and jackknifing their bodies sideways into extravagant dives, I was one of the few able to sustain a seemingly effortless floating position.

Later, before Dad died, he convinced me that floating in the lake was a great way to relax from my university studies and exams. I was amazed at how all the cares of my world seemed to drift away with the waves and swells.

He himself would head to the lake in the early evenings, after the Kerby Lodgers had retired to their cabins for dinner and games. Dad would have aching muscles from scouting the woods, felling trees, and maintaining the property. But Lake Michigan, he claimed, was his "cure-all" for everything.

If only that were true.

If only Dad, and then Mum, wouldn't have succumbed to a powerful strain of flu and pneumonia—one after the other. I'd give anything to have Dad here with me now, so I could talk with this wise man about my life.

Opening my tear-filled eyes, I gazed up at the bluest sky, and saw large white clouds moving at a good clip. At this pace, the clouds would be hovering over Lake Huron by nightfall.

I'd been to Lake Huron, which had its own charms, a time or two.

If Lake Michigan was the prettiest girl at the prom, the wild untamed beauty that all the boys were waiting to dance with, Lake Huron was its demure cousin. A Plain Jane sweetheart that promised to never stray, or break any hearts.

In fact, it was lovely swimming off of Lake Huron's Michigan coast. That is, once I got beyond the painful rocks, and walked a good quarter of a mile past the shallows.

But it's *this* lake that draws the sportsmen, the anglers, and the very rich.

That wasn't always the case. Back in the 1800s, the population of Michigan exploded tenfold as the mines and lumber, and then the fledgling auto industry demanded many laborers. Immigrants from Scandinavian countries were joined by people from Europe and the UK, and they all scrambled to settle in.

On their precious days off, these new residents would travel to "camp" near one of Michigan's abundant lakes and rivers—to cool off and bathe with a swim, and catch their dinner on the end of a fishing rod or stick.

While the children napped in the shade of the trees, the adults would sit and tell stories of their past lives. All except the Irish, who thought it bad luck to bring tales of their homeland into a new country.

After a time, they starting building small cabins and modest shanties— camps, they called them—to return to time and again, and get away from the congested cities.

"What's the difference between a camp, a cabin, and a cottage?" I asked my dad.

"A cabin is a fancy camp," he said, "and a cottage is a fancy cabin."

And some of the homes on Lake Michigan, he went on to tell me, are beyond category. They could only be called *sand castles,* these so-called cottage-mansions that exceed millions of dollars, and thousands of square feet.

Some are year-round homes, and others are summer getaways for captains of industry and Hollywood moguls alike. Enjoyed for a few weeks, and then closed up again.

"Look for the coffee can," my decorator Jack told me when I asked him about camps and cabins. His grandfather had told him that if there was an old Maxwell House coffee can on the table, filled with playing cards, it was a camp.

But surely the Atwater's didn't have a simple camp, or a cabin. From what I witnessed, Lilian and her husband Skip likely had a cottage worth millions. And Lilian was going to protect her little sand castle, and young prince not-so-charming, with all her might.

No doubt, she would soon discover I had indeed married into Chicago Mayne money. That would surely result in an invitation to the club, or to cocktails—a minefield I wasn't sure how to navigate.

And no doubt she was scurrying around, trying to connect the dots between her acquaintances and Bella's family in Atlanta.

Who did Tad work for—was the hospital director Skip's frat brother?

Which old Atlanta family was Selby from?

Oh, the networking, posturing, and elbow rubbing was all so exhausting and unnecessary, and my least favorite part of this particular Lake Michigan culture. A culture I had been immune to until now.

In spite of the cool water, I felt a slow burn at Lilian Atwater's audacity. As if she were determining my niece Bella's value based on my marriage, or the company Bella's parents kept.

Closing my eyes, I tried to concentrate on the water and the wind, while I planned my escape. I would hitch a ride with the clouds.

To Lake Huron.

21

Sammies from the Rusty Nail were brilliant.
And we all know vacation carbs don't count.
-KERBY LODGE GUEST BOOK-

"I'm sorry that I knocked over your spirits—here's a gift card to the Rusty Nail, with my sincere apology. I hope that you can build a lovely picnic basket and forgive my clumsiness." This I said to guests in Room 3, as they nodded in confusion.

Their wine cost less than $20, and the gift card was for $100—but I knew that merely replacing the wine could not replace the sentimental value of whatever life event they had been toasting before they sealed it up.

It wasn't enough to *replace.* I had to regain their trust and good will.

I did the same with my guests in Room 5, explaining that I had spilled wine on their crackers and cheese, and hoped they could forgive my blunder by shopping for new goodies with a hefty gift card.

I would make little profit from these two rooms on this day. But with lodges, cabins, and B&Bs multiplying along the coast—thanks to a recession-provoked dip in property costs—I had to be as competitive as possible.

Ten days into their stay, the girls seemed to have neutralized their anger and disdain at being on Lake Michigan, and not at their home in Atlanta. Wren helped Jennifer at Carriage House Treasures on the days when she was open. And was now placing the lunch orders each day for guests who wanted sandwiches from the Rusty Nail.

She also had a little shadow. Cody Gray seemed to take a liking to Wren, and followed her around the grounds. Wren gave Cody rides in the golf cart that we use to clean the cabins, and pushed him on the swings. Sometimes they sat in the shade, sipping juice boxes.

Sadly, I hardly ever saw Cody's father with the boy, and rarely saw the Gray's together as a family. A time or two, Joy Gray took Cody to the beach, or for a walk in the woods. Stuart seemed to prefer sitting on an Adirondack chair in the shade of the lodge, reading or napping.

He was indulging in the activities of a single man, a man without children, and it made me angry. "Selfish, selfish man," I thought but didn't say, as I passed Stuart on the grounds. I wondered, could he not see all the other fathers—the other families walking to the beach together? They were laughing and tossing footballs and catching frisbees, talking about their antics and adventures on the water.

I saw one dad walking next to his adolescent son as they came up after swimming, and the dad was playfully ruffling the son's hair over and over again. The kid pretended he wanted his dad to stop, but his face and his grin said otherwise—he was soaking in his father's attention like a houseplant in the sun.

Cody, meanwhile, often sat on the beach by himself. He played in the sand and watched other guests swimming in Lake Michigan, no doubt longing to be in the water. And as much as Wren wanted to, I insisted that she not take Cody in the lake in lieu of his absentee parents. It was too much responsibility for a young girl.

She wasn't used to the strong currents.

On more than one occasion, I saw the young boy occupying his time by watching a pair of loons near the shore with rapt attention. Just as I used to when I was his age, and still do, when I can spare the time.

When he was alive, Fitz was an advocate in the community for keeping the shoreline as rugged and natural as possible, so as not to disturb the habitats for these, and other beautiful creatures. While other developers along Lake Michigan seem to favor long expanses of white sand beaches, not reeds and marshes.

"People want to turn Michigan into Florida," Fitz told me once when I was a girl. I didn't understand it then, but I'm beginning to.

The natural terrain of Lake Michigan has coves and reeds, marshes, trees and shrubs. The loons depend on these reeds and marshes, and the tall grasses, to find the fish and frogs they need to survive. And to protect their precious eggs from predators.

A loon's nest is close to the shore. If they detect an intruder, they will stand up in the water and frantically flap their wings in a wild and feathery warning. This water dance, as it's called, is meant to be a display of unbridled anger.

We will do whatever it takes to protect our little one, the loon is saying.

But it's a beautiful sight to behold. Especially given that a loon's wingspan can reach a full five feet. Sadly, though, if the intruder does not back down, a loon might get too worked up, resulting in a seizure, or even its own death.

I tried to imagine being so protective over anything, that I would flap my wings to death in order to prevent it from being harmed. The Gray's certainly weren't working very hard to protect their little chick—Cody was wandering all over Kerby Lodge without anyone *water dancing* over him.

Anyone except Wren, that is.

As for the stolen items from the guest fridge, I held Bella responsible for her and Max's actions by tasking her with washing and drying bedding each day. My usual helper from town was on vacation, and I had planned on hiring a fill-in. Instead, I told Bella she could pitch in and save me that expense.

She took the news in stride, as if she thought it a fair sentence. I was proud of her for that, and knew her parents would be, too.

Watching her trying to fold sheets out of the dryer was both amusing and excruciating—she was like a little child learning to wrap a gift with sticky peanut butter hands. The fitted sheets almost had her in tears the first few days, and I felt guilty.

"Let me help," I said. "These are challenging for everyone."

As I picked a sheet out of the dryer, Bella glared at me, but didn't speak.

"Raya taught me how to fold when I was a little girl," I said, "she started me on small washrags, and then I moved up to pillowcases." I told Bella how glad I was to be able to fold by the time I went off to University.

"My clothes always looked the best of anyone in my dorm," I said.

I was aware, as I spoke, that everything I told her was grist for the mill; it was information she could use to make jokes at my expense, or throw back in my face.

To her credit, she didn't respond in the negative, though I found myself cringing in anticipation of her next verbal attack. I even went so far as to craft some of the mean comments she could make, and played them out in my head.

No wonder Dad got out of here as soon as he could.

Or, *hooray, I learned to fold a washrag this summer.*

Would being around this girl ever get easier?

22

We noticed your rates went up this year.
But Kerby Lodge is still cheaper than therapy.
-KERBY LODGE GUEST BOOK-

Maybe it's because Bella refrained from saying ugly remarks while she folded the sheets that I allowed Max to return to Kerby Lodge. She asked me on his behalf if he could come and swim again. Maybe they could take the kayaks out for a short ride along the shore, "with Wren too, of course," she suggested, and perhaps grill a few hotdogs before he left.

"To return his hospitality," Bella said.

I had to work so hard not to roll my eyes.

For I'd seen Max's hospitality. It was always at the expense of others, I was dying to point out—my expense, his mother's, and my valued guests. But I held my tongue.

Whatever my answer, Bella said, Max was coming to speak with me.

"I would like to apologize, Mrs. Mayne," Max said later that afternoon, as we stood in the great room of the lodge. He was wearing his faded blue Oxford shirt again, and his most sincere puppy dog face—the one he would no doubt take to Yale the next year and try on his female professors.

I didn't know the paper was due today!

It was a good face, a practiced and contrite face, but all I could see as he talked was the smirk he wore when Daniel and I found him on the deck of the A-Frame a few days ago.

80

"Taking the wine and the food from your guests was my idea," he went on, "and I am sorry for causing Bella to get in trouble, and for damaging your trust."

Oh, this kid was good.

But out of the corner of my eye, I saw Bella watching from the apartment kitchen. I could tell from her face that she had no idea how I was going to respond, and neither did I, really. Until I heard Raya's brogue in my head:

Say soory and carry on, lass.

That's the principle I was raised on, because we all make mistakes. Apologize, try to do better, and carry on. But as I was about to speak, Daniel came into the great room where Max and I stood, and planted himself like a tree—a sequoia—next to me.

Max gulped and his eyes grew wide.

"I… was apologizing to Mrs. Mayne," Max said, his voice breaking a little as he tried to hold eye contact with Daniel.

Daniel nodded. "So I gather," the tall tree said to young sapling.

Max turned his gaze back to me, where he undoubtedly thought he'd find a more sympathetic face, but Daniel spoke instead, commanding Max's full attention.

His voice was low, but strong and clear as he towered over the boy.

"You've been given all measure of toys and entertainment in your young life," Daniel said, "but lad, the fine people of this town, my family, and especially my nieces, are not your playthings. Are we perfectly clear?"

Max nodded quickly, and then decided it may not be enough.

"Yes sir," Max whispered.

Walking with Daniel to his car a few minutes later, I could tell he was reluctant to leave. But he had to head out for work.

"I hate to go," he said, putting his suitcase in his trunk, "with Luke away."

I laughed a little at that.

"Do we need a bouncer at Kerby Lodge?" I asked him. "An enforcer to strong-arm spoiled boys who wanted to swim at our beach?"

"I hear you laughing, Kaker," he said, "but you've got three young women under your roof now. And you yourself haven't been looking so good since you got back from your travels."

"Thanks!" I said with false indignation, but surprised that anyone noticed my jet lag. It made me wonder if Luke had noticed.

"You know what I mean, Kay," he said.

Daniel Mayne was not prone to frivolous thoughts, so I tried to take him seriously. I hadn't been myself since we got home, and I had a lot of responsibility on my shoulders all of a sudden—with no one to share it.

Growing up at Kerby Lodge, we were a large family, all looking out for each other.

For twelve years after Mum and Dad died, I still had my aunt and uncle. Though I could hardly consider Zeke a strong male presence. In his plaid golf shorts, with black socks pulled up to his knobby knees, he was more comfort to me than protection.

"If I trusted Max, it would be another matter," Daniel said, "but a leopard can't change its spots. And I don't trust the boy to not cause trouble for you."

I wasn't sure I did either, but I didn't want Bella and Wren to be bored at Kerby Lodge. Or hate Kerby Lodge, as she said she did.

"How is it," I asked Daniel, changing the conversation, "that you and Luke were raised in a privileged home—but you both turned out to be nice? Not entitled, like Max Atwater."

Daniel smiled. "They never told us we were wealthy," he said. "Except for a great vacation every summer, we had no idea. Luke and I were held accountable for doing our chores, doing our homework, and writing letters to our aunties and grams. Nan volunteered us every week to shovel a neighbor's driveway or deliver groceries to someone in need, and we worked for the things we wanted."

I smiled at the image of the earnest, industrious young Mayne brothers, and suddenly missed Luke terribly.

Daniel went on to tell me that if he and Luke ever started to put on airs, which was one of Nan's phrases, their parents would cart them to all nine locations of Mayne Fine Jewelers and have them clean the bathrooms.

"We'll give the cleaning crew a paid day off," their dad would say.

82

23

"I came to say I'm really sorry."

I walked into Carriage House Treasures the next morning as Jennifer opened her doors. She was plugging in the old Methodist Church coffee urn that I had given her last spring for her grand opening; the one I bought at the church's *Our Blessings* sale, and used myself for years.

As put off as I was at Max's lukewarm apology, it brought home my own guilt at blasting Jennifer. She had only been trying to protect my vacation, and had done no harm.

Maybe if Jennifer forgave me, and I prayed she could, she'd let me have a cup of her coffee. The stuff from the new urn had not tasted right since I returned, though I longed for it every day while I was away.

Patrick was with Jennifer, and they both eyed me neutrally. He had been dating Jennifer for nearly two years now, and was her former EMT partner. Since the county added four more professionals, they each had new co-workers.

I had come to love Patrick and his boisterous, fun-loving friendship. He had stayed friends with Daniel, and also fully welcomed Luke when he came on the scene. Luke and Patrick even collaborated this past school year on safety talks for the middle schoolers on a variety of topics. The talks went over so well, they were expanding them in the coming year.

I would have a lot of explaining to do if Luke came home to find that I'd alienated all of our good friends while he was away. And honestly, I had messed up.

"Jennifer, you're my best and oldest friend, and I treated you badly," I said.

Jennifer turned to look at me, and she had tears welling up in her eyes.

"No," she said, "it was my mistake not to call you in Europe. This is your lodge, not mine, and you trusted me to keep you informed. I only meant to help you!"

We hugged and all was forgiven on both sides.

Say soory and carry on!

"Now, can I please have a cup of your coffee, and take a look at your new inventory?" I asked my now smiling friend, as if no time at all had passed between us.

Sitting on a vintage stepladder by Jennifer's cash register, I sipped coffee from a hand-thrown Carriage House Treasures mug and took a good look around as the breeze off the water cooled my bare arms.

Her repurposed and refinished furniture and other treasures were nestled in a magical display, complete with twinkling lights and fragrant pine boughs. One dresser was painted a pretty lake blue, with white hand-painted flowers up and down the drawers. Another was antiqued in white, with stenciled *fleurs* and swirls on the top.

"My, you've taken these pieces to a new level, Jen," I said. And judging from the percentage she had been giving me as rent every month, she was finding an audience.

Patrick had gone to the top of the road to place a large sign near the entrance of the lodge, telling passers-by that the store was open. Customers began driving down the lodge road almost immediately after. Earlier, I had put a few orange cones in the parking pad to block off the circle drive, giving young Cody and other children at the lodge a safe place to ride their little bikes and scooters—away from incoming cars.

Years ago, this carriage house was stuffed to the rafters with bikes and trikes and wagons—and my brother Tad spent his days keeping everything in top working order for our youngest guests. Sadly, I hadn't been able to maintain the toys, and let everything go to rust.

Last spring, with Jennifer and Patrick's help, we had a massive estate sale and sold nearly everything, except for a few old bikes that Jack and Stace used in their cabin décor.

I do keep my eyes out for toys when I pass yard sales in town, so I have a few riding toys to occupy the kids. And the new plastic toys don't need to be maintained—just hosed off.

Young Cody was enjoying a scooter that was just his size, but one he would quickly grow out of. A few other kids were having fun too, so this little boy wasn't alone, I was glad to see. I hardly ever saw his parents playing with him.

The boy follows Wren around the lodge, and she is so good-natured that she doesn't seem to mind. One nagging thought was that Wren would tell my brother I allowed her to become an unpaid nanny.

The Grays were our guests, though, and I was unsure how to handle the situation—or even if it was a situation. "*Och Mum,*" I would say to Raya, if I could pick up the phone and call her, "did you ever see guests so aloof... who left their wee ones to their own devices?"

After showing a few pieces to her customers, Jennifer came and sat down next to me on her own stool. Patrick helped customers load furniture into their cars, and then moved displays around to fill in the gaps.

"I'm scrambling to keep up, Kay," she confessed. "I'll have to be busier than ever this winter, to replenish my inventory."

"As long as it makes you happy, Jennifer," I said, "but it shouldn't be stressful."

This had been Jennifer's dream for years.

"I hope she still has a minute or two for me," Patrick chimed in, pulling up a folding chair. "I hardly see her as it is."

Jennifer smiled, but she almost looked sad. Patrick must love Jennifer a great deal to spend his days off moving frilly little pieces of furniture here and there for her—instead of being out on the lake. As Patrick and Jennifer reached out to take each other's hand, I said to all three of us: "Be careful what we wish for, I suppose, because we just might get it."

And as I looked over at Cody and the other children, a dark shadow of a thought passed through my mind as I realized how the traffic from Saturday weddings would affect my youngest guests next summer. There wouldn't be any safe patch of driveway for them to play on. And how would Carriage House Treasures remain open on wedding days, when my narrow road would be bumper to bumper with incoming guests?

When the time came, I'd let Jennifer know about my destination wedding plans, but not right now. Not after she'd just forgiven my most recent trespasses.

Even as I planned to trespass against her.

24

I got 99 problems, but this lake ain't one
-KERBY LODGE GUEST BOOK-

"Max says you're loaded," Wren was saying, "is that true Aunt Kay?"

My iced tea lodged in my throat as Wren surprised me, and I nearly spit onto the linen-covered dinner table. I set my fork down. The baked mac and cheese I'd ordered at Mitch's restaurant would have to wait for a minute.

Mitch himself had sat the girls and I near the window, nearly as soon as we arrived. Bypassing a dozen other guests who were there before us.

As we sat down, I introduced Bella and Wren to my long-time friend, the owner of the popular restaurant on the waterfront. Mitch charmed them with his bright smile, tanned face and silver hair. They were the perfect belles, answering his queries about Tad, and smiling with delight as he remarked how each of them bore a striking resemblance to Raya and Fitz, respectively.

The girls beamed at Mitch as they hung on his every word.

"Your grandparents, and your father, and aunt, are some of my favorite people," Mitch told them, "and now I'm pleased to welcome a third generation of Kerby's. Imagine that!"

"Imagine that," I echoed.

As Mitch walked off to make his rounds of the dining tables, I smiled, knowing there would be warm slices of his cherry pie showing up at the

end of the meal, whether we ordered them or not. Mitch cultivated his own orchard, and had a thriving pie business that kept him busy year-round.

"Max said what, Wren?" I asked, in true surprise.

She smiled a little at my response.

Was it just my nieces, I wondered, or do teenagers in general enjoy saying things for shock value? Do they all wait until you have something in your mouth to choke on?

"*He* said… that his *mama* said… that *you* married into a lot of Mayne money," she explained. "And that Mayne money is *fundin'* your renovations, and your *weddin'* venue, and especially Gram's Mid-Century Modern makeover, which *she* said costs a pretty penny."

Wren's sweet southern accent almost made her words sound charming. But it was not a charming sentiment, by any stretch. That woman! Lilian Atwater was talking about things she knew nothing about. As if I'd married Luke Mayne so I could have Mayne money to play with. After working so hard to recover from the recession the nation was still enduring.

"Oh, she did, did she?" I said, biting into my mac and cheese. It was good, with the crunchy parmesan crisps baked on the top. I could eat this every day of my life.

The girls, I knew, were waiting for me to respond. Blow up, even. And as much as I wanted to, I took the time to think on it, taking a few more bites of dinner.

"What do you think Wren?" I finally asked, looking right at her. "Does that sound like something I would do?" She gazed at me, but didn't answer.

"How about Luke—you girls have spent time with him," I said, drawing Bella into the conversation, "does he seem like a man who'd fund a lavish lifestyle with Mayne money?"

Both girls seemed to relax their tense shoulders as they came to the same conclusion, that Max and his mother were off target.

"I will tell you the absolute transparent truth," I said, "but what I'm going to say is not Atwater business. This is Kerby family business—and you, remember, are Kerby's."

I had their full attention at that, and they both nodded solemnly.

"Your grandparents were very smart, hard-working people," I said. "They worked for years and saved every penny they could. That's how they purchased the Kerby property outright, without any mortgage. They could have lived in it as their home," I went on, "but they still had so much energy and a love for life, that they created a lodge to share with others."

I told Bella and Wren how Fitz and Raya spent their final years raising their father and me in the most beautiful place in the world, and gave us a strong start.

"Your dad and I were loved beyond measure, just as you two are. We both had great educations, thanks to our parents and their work ethic," I said. "While they couldn't get Tad all the way through medical school, they supported him as much as they could."

The girls nodded. They loved their dad and were proud of him, I knew.

"When I inherited the lodge, it was still a profitable business," I said. "But for several years after Fitz and Raya died, I struggled with depression. Then the economy took a bad turn, and Kerby Lodge was in real trouble. I nearly lost everything."

As the girls looked on in rapt attention, I told them how it was Daniel Mayne who helped me give it a new life—though he and I were not friends at first. And how I fell in love with his brother Luke through our phone conversations and the confidences we shared.

"The Mayne brothers gave me courage. They believed in me," I said. I told the girls how I married Luke Mayne thinking he had nothing more than a duffel bag of clothing to his name.

"He and I decided early on that Kerby Lodge must be sustainable as a business, or else we would not keep running it," I told them. "That's why we all pitch in, folding sheets and cleaning cabins. We keep expenses low, and profits as high as possible."

"But what about the renovations?" Wren asked.

"That's a valid question Wren," I said. "I have a fund that I set aside from the profits to funnel back into the property—to invest in its upkeep. Which is substantial, as I'm sure you can imagine. A single project can wipe out that fund, because of the size of the property. But except for taking a few trees down this summer, I'm not tapping into any of that *Kerby* money."

"Oh?" Bella was suddenly curious.

"No," I said. "Since Gram's house isn't income generating, meaning we don't ever rent it out, Luke and I used our own income for the updates, in lieu of not having to pay for housing. But aside from the furnace, it's paint and flooring. We're even re-using Gram's furniture."

I went on to tell them that the insurance claim would cover many of the repairs caused by the leak. Same as the A-Frame.

"Isn't the A-Frame… income generating?" Wren wanted to know.

"It used to be," I said. "Daniel was the last person to rent it, and that was two years ago. Since then, I kind of think of it as his. He probably does too, but that may have to change."

The girls nodded, as I thought once again about talking to Daniel.

"Anyway," I said, pulling myself back from my thoughts, "that's a long way of saying that I married Luke for love."

His parents may have money, I told them, but it's not our money—and may never be. With all of Nan and Sperry's charitable foundations, we may never see Mayne money in our lifetime. I hoped we didn't.

I told them I'd rather have Nan and Sperry in our lives for a very long time, rather than any inheritance that may come our way. And I meant it.

"Trust me," I said, "an inheritance can't replace the people who leave it to us."

The girls seemed satisfied, and happy that I had spoken to them about family business, as equals. I didn't mention, because it really was none of their business, the large wedding gift from the Mayne's, or Luke's trust fund. Or the fact that Tad and I would be co-heirs to Zeke and June's significant holdings someday.

Hopefully not for a long, long time.

I also didn't mention that property values along the Lake Michigan coastline seemed to be going up again, along with an increased economic confidence. Meaning, I could probably sell Kerby Lodge in a few years, and be "loaded" myself, if I wanted to.

But there was more I did want to say.

"I want you to know that if Max had been right, there would be no shame in it," I told the girls. "If Luke had a lot of money and wanted to spend it on me, and on Kerby Lodge, that's his business. And his decision to make."

They nodded.

"But that's not our reality," I said.

Bella and Wren were so young still, but I hoped they would grow in their confidence and sense of loyalty. To where they could say "that's family business" to the likes of Max Atwater—a boy going on a fishing expedition into our private lives.

But he is just a boy. So, who chartered it?

I wondered.

25

Beach you to the lake...
-KERBY LODGE GUEST BOOK-

Sadly, I knew it was just a matter of time until I heard again from Lilian Atwater, since this social climber had indeed confirmed my connection with the wealthy Chicago Mayne's. Sure enough, upon returning from dinner, she called to invite me and the girls to their home the next afternoon for a "social."

"The young people, of course, will enjoy some water fun," she said, "while us old crones have a drinkie or two on the deck."

Ugh.

This was the last thing I wanted to do. But Bella had just begun to speak to me without shooting daggers out of her eyes, and we'd be back to the drawing board if I said no.

"I, uh..." I stammered.

"Perfect. Until tomorrow then," Lilian said in her choked, staccato voice—as if her starched, popped collar was stabbing her in the neck.

She hung up before I had the chance to decline, or think up a valid excuse, so that was that. I had a date with the old crones. I wondered if, at age 36, I'd be the youngest old crone. And if I'd be the only old crone sticking with Coke—my drinkie of choice.

The other invitation that came an hour later was one I actually welcomed. Stace Wildberry invited us to their grandfather's camp for a cookout and lake party.

In two days.

Their mother Beth would be there, which I knew I'd enjoy. Beth is the owner of Wildberry Consignment Shop, the resale store that helped me redesign my entire lodge for pennies on the dollar the previous year. I'd been back a time or two, and once mentioned that my favorite "find" was her twins, who, with their interior design degrees, had been a tremendous help to Kerby Lodge.

She, in turn, told me how much my lodge redesign had helped to launch her son and daughter's budding careers. A few of their social media posts—traversing furniture to snowy cabins on sleds, for instance—went viral, and led to a flurry of new business.

Would the twins' father be at the cookout? I silently wondered about this. I thought it funny that he was never mentioned.

"Jack and I will make sure your nieces have a great time, Kay," Stace said. "Gramps doesn't allow any motors, only kayaks and canoes."

Stace assured me that I would adore their grandfather, who said he was looking forward to meeting me, and showing me his place on the water. Which, she said, was even more rustic than my own lodge had been, before the renovation.

"This truly sounds like the best invitation I've had all summer, Stace," I said.

I only wished Luke were home to join us.

After firming up the time, and agreeing to bring a fresh caprese salad with a balsamic reduction drizzle, I said farewell to Stace. At no point in our conversation did our stalled Mid-Century Modern renovation come up, but this wasn't the time.

"Your dance card is filling up," Aunt June said when I told her of the two calls I'd received earlier that day.

"I never wanted a full dance card, June," I replied. "Social engagements only interfere with my life, and my time at the lake."

"That's not a life, Kaker," she said, "say yes to both, and show the girls some fun."

I had called June to see if they could make a trip north for my Labor Day weekend cookout—my new family tradition. But I wasn't a fan of her tone. I had too many people bossing me around this summer.

Besides, the longer we stayed on the phone, the more the likelihood that I'd blab about my plans to turn Kerby Lodge into a wedding venue. She would not approve, I was sure; plus, she'd have a million questions that I wasn't prepared to answer.

"Do I hear a phone ringing June?" I said. "Is that a canasta game calling you?"

Luke and I talked nearly every day while he was away. Mostly small talk about his conference speakers and workshops, and my time with Bella and Wren. But there wasn't much to talk about there.

The girls may have been slightly bored, but kept somewhat busy. Wren played with Cody Gray and placed sandwich orders, and sometimes helped Jennifer at the carriage house. Bella stretched her lackluster effort at folding sheets for longer than necessary.

Max came by many afternoons. After eyeing me warily, and searching the grounds for Daniel's car, he'd make his way to the beach to swim and sunbathe with Bella, Wren, and whatever kids from town showed up.

It seemed harmless enough.

Luke was adamant that Bella shouldn't leave the lodge with Max, and that I should keep a close eye on them when he was here. I thought he was sounding a little preachy, too.

"Yes, I've got this, Luke," I said, trying to hide the impatience from my tone. "The kids swim. Sometimes they play cards and board games on the porch, and they eat snacks."

The elephant in the room that we both avoided was the comment he had made about me not being Raya.

And my sharp rebuttal that he was not Fitz.

26

There should be sympathy cards for people who
have to leave Kerby Lodge and go back home.
-KERBY LODGE GUEST BOOK-

Social clubs on and around Lake Michigan are numerous.

The old ones are steeped in history. Several began as religious communities in the mid 1800s. Multi-level gingerbread homes were built near large meeting halls, where women in long white summer dresses, and men in beige linen suits, once gathered to hear speakers and preachers during their vacation.

Many lakeshore associations carry on these traditions still.

Others have unashamedly transitioned into exclusive yacht, golf, and country clubs with full dining rooms, tennis courts, and private beaches— where the only religion is "thou shalt not" allow non-members in during the high tourist season.

The original houses stand three and four full stories tall, and are built of clapboard, ship beams, and leftover lumber from a bygone era. These turreted homes have been passed down through multiple generations and rarely come on the market. As a result, newer associations have sprung up along the coast. Emulating the traditions and rules of the originals, minus the religious edification.

In an exclusive harbor town north of Petoskey, one original association has a rule that the only thing sacred are the months of July and August— there will be no hammers and saws heard or seen during this time. All repairs and construction must be completed by the end of June, and can commence again after Labor Day.

Another is more tradition than a rule—and involves a plastic pink flamingo.

One home in the association places the flamingo in their front yard, signaling to others that they will be hosting cocktails on that day. The women making a grab for the bird are the most anxious to show off their kitchen renovations, or new guest house. Maybe a freshly decorated sleeping porch.

During the party, other guests discretely jockey for the right to host the next night. And so on, through Labor Day.

I wasn't sure what the tradition was in the Atwater's *nouveau riche* neighborhood, but it was clear by all the cars in the driveway that Lilian had grabbed the flamingo.

Cottage names burnished on discreet signs are also familiar sites in our communities, especially along the lake. As I drove to Lilian's social, I passed the *Gone Coastal, Shore Enuff,* and *SeaBatical.* I went past our host's driveway initially, as there was a line of cars waiting to valet park and I didn't react quickly enough.

I turned around in the driveway of *Baydream Believer,* trying not to take out the mailbox belonging to *Anchors Away.*

Bella probably could have shown me their house, but she was busy hiding her face from the embarrassment she felt, riding in my vintage Jeep instead of the new SUV.

When Wren and I were walking to the car earlier, I did not see my eldest niece.

"She's waiting in the new car, Aunt Kay," Wren said.

"Bella," I called to her, "are you coming?"

The look as she got out of one car and had to climb into the other was nothing but sheer horror, but I was not about to posture for my family— or for anybody, for that matter. Least of all Max's mother.

What Bella apparently didn't know was how my 1970s Jeep had increased in value through the years. Even now, in the depths of the recession, I was fielding offers way above what my parents paid for it brand new. My travels were mainly local, same as my parents before me, and the miles on this baby were ridiculously low—increasing its appeal.

But Bella and Wren couldn't help but overhear the college-aged valet whistle "sweet" when he took my keys. And I know they both caught the smile on his suntanned face when he jumped in behind the wheel, because I saw their eyebrows raise.

These two young beauties, no doubt, thought they should be the ones being whistled at, instead of the old Jeep they rode in on.

I shouldn't have been surprised that Lilian and Skip Atwater made a play on their own name, calling their cottage the *At th' Water*. Frankly, I wouldn't be surprised if Lilian had married Skip for his name, as much as for his money.

It was an unimposing summer home from the entrance—gray cedar shake exterior with navy nautical-design shutters—but as the girls and I got closer to the pale blue door, I could see that it was built like an iceberg. And we were only seeing the tip. The bulk of the beautiful house was carved into the hillside and sloped towards the lake.

Best viewed from the Atwater's 40-foot yacht.

Inside the foyer, there were brass anchors on the wall to hang windbreakers and beach bags, and a rattan basket filled with assorted flip flops and sandals. A wooden sign pointing towards the water said simply: *Beach*.

I wondered if they also had a sign that read: *Only Dead Fish Go With the Flow*—or if they might want one? Maybe I should have brought Lilian a hostess gift.

"Bella, darling, and Wren!" Lilian gushed as we came in. "Aren't you girls a breath of fresh air to us stale old golf widows, right Kay?" she said this without actually looking at me.

"Let me introduce you."

Lilian whisked the girls into her main room that overlooked the water, and to waiting groups of older and overly tanned women wearing this year's Coldwater Creek tunics. I wandered over to a bar and asked for a well-iced Coke.

I hadn't known what to wear, but didn't feel out of place in a short navy skirt and bleached white Oxford shirt, tied at the waist. That is, until I saw the bartender, and realized we wore matching outfits. I suppose if the party was dull, I could grab a tray and clear some plates.

At least I had taken a little extra time with my hair. And I wore my silver and sea glass jewelry that Luke sent me two Christmases ago—before we'd ever met.

I think I actually looked nice, for the first time in weeks, and wished I were out on a date with Luke instead of in a room full of strangers. We could be at Mitch's, ordering the day's fresh catch, watching the sun sink down over the water.

Would we ever get to enjoy summer together on Lake Michigan? Not with our current schedules and demands.

"Now, Kay, I know you're not a golf widow," I heard a voice saying. And standing next to me, much to my happy surprise, was Sue Spondike. Sue and I graduated from high school together. She was married to Chip, who was also an old friend, and my elusive tree remover.

Chip plowed the snow off the Kerby Lodge driveway for years. But it's a good thing he didn't rely on the Kerby's to pay his bills, because year after year he gave me the "old friend rate" of next to nothing—he probably spent more in gas, I realized. But he would not budge.

"Your father was a friend of mine when I started my business," Chip told me once. It made me smile to think of Fitzwilliam Kerby dispensing advice to a young Chip, while standing in the woods on an early morning. Each with their coffee mugs in hand.

Now that I close the inn down for the winter, Chip's invoices were non-issues.

But he didn't need me. His main income was earned in the summer, off his growing fleet of landscaping trucks, and a thriving business beautifying the yards of wealthy cottage owners.

I was sure the Atwater's were clients.

"Sue!" We gave each other a warm hug and went to find a couple of chairs. She pointed to the group of teens on the dock, getting ready to board the Atwater jet skis. "The girl in the red bikini is Patti Lee, our oldest. She turned 16 this summer," Sue was saying.

"I can't believe you have a teenager, Sue," I said. I knew their youngest was a fourth grader last year, because he was in Rhonda Ellis' class that I substituted for while she was on maternity leave.

"That's what you get when you marry a year out of high school," she said, good naturedly, "while you, newlywed Kay Mayne, went to the other extreme."

"I did," I said, laughing, "and you're right, I'm not a gold widow. Luke is at a conference, getting ready for the school year."

"Something I'm not ready to think about," Sue laughed.

She went on to say how thankful the community was for Luke Mayne, vice principal of the middle school. "The kids and parents both love him," she said, "and that's rare."

I nodded. That was the conclusion I had come to as well, but wondered if it was my own partiality and pride in Luke that made me imagine his popularity.

I asked Sue how business was going for her this summer. She had inherited her parents' string of Spondike Gift Shops along the coast, and had fought like mad to keep them open in the past few years, during the worst of the recession.

"I diversified my inventory," she said, "and do a lot of the work myself." Which made her sad, she told me, as the Spondike companies have long enjoyed a reputation as a premier seasonal employer; helping kids earn tuition money, and senior citizens subsidize their costly prescriptions.

Just as Sue was asking me about Kerby Lodge, the sound of motors captured our attention. We looked out to see three jet skis racing off towards the sun. Bella sat behind Max on one, Wren sat with Patti Lee on another, and two more kids were on a third. Thankfully they were all wearing life jackets, because Max was going very fast.

The others tried to keep up.

27

Skipped my HS reunion to come here.
Go to the head of the class!
-KERBY LODGE GUEST BOOK-

"Teenagers make my head hurt," Sue said, and we smiled at each other.

"They make my stomach hurt," I confessed. "But only for a few more weeks, and then they go back to Atlanta."

Sue knew all about my nieces. Maybe the girls could spend more time with Patti Lee in the coming weeks, and not so much with Max. I felt a wave of gratitude that Sue was a guest at this party, and that we had renewed our friendship.

As if on cue, Lilian shouted our names from across the room. "Sue and Kay, that's enough of your little *tete-a-tete*," she said with a slur, trying to sound fun, but only managing to sound loud and edgy. "Come and mingle with us *old gals*."

Sue and I stole a glance at each other while getting up, and I was sure she was thinking the same thing I was—*look out, Lilian Atwater is half in the bag*.

Skip Atwater arrived after a full day of golf, appearing tired and strained. The other men that came in with him looked as if they'd enjoyed their afternoon. Sue's husband Chip was among the men who found and greeted their wives, then added to the laughter.

Skip found Lilian, but only by zeroing in on her across the room, and narrowing his eyes. She was telling a story that she found terribly funny. Few others did, judging by their body language, and the way they were searching for an exit strategy.

98

I couldn't tell if Skip was frowning at his wife's unsavory choice of words, or the volume of her voice. But he exhaled deeply, and took a few long strides to be by her side. Putting his arm around her, I watched him dig his tanned fingers into her ribs in such a way that she got whatever message he was sending.

"Skipper," she said, in a voice that had gone from bawdy to whiney in an instant. Or maybe she was trying to sound romantic. It was hard to tell, and frankly I didn't want to know.

I caught the attention of the girls, who had joined the fray of adults. They each had a small plate of canapes and fruit—I'm sure they were hungry after being on the water.

I knew that many in the crowd would be gravitating *en masse* to the yacht club for dinner, and I didn't want to deal with an insistent invitation.

"Let's go," I mouthed to Wren, and she nodded to let me know she too was eager to go back to the lodge. She tugged on the sleeve of Bella's swimsuit coverup, and after initial resistance, Bella walked with Wren towards the door. She was wearing her sunglasses so I couldn't see her eyes, but she looked as if she needed to lie down.

"Too much sun?" I asked Bella and Wren. It was easy to overdo it out on the lake. The breezes and the air from the jet ski masked the beating summer sun, and many a vacationer had their trip ruined by excessive sunburn or sun stroke. Or dehydration.

The girls were ahead of me. I told Wren to ask the valet to pull my Jeep out for us. I wanted to grab a few bottles of water from the buffet for the girls to drink on the way home.

As I made my way towards the door, I debated whether I should go say goodbye to my hostess instead of slipping out, but I opted to keep walking, and send her my apologies in the morning. I passed Sue and Chip, and gave them a small wave on my way out.

I wanted to ask Chip when he was coming to cut down the pines, but saw that he and Sue were in a close huddle with Patti Lee, and intent on their conversation. Maybe mine weren't the only teens who had too much sun exposure. And as if to support that, I came outside to find Bella bent over a hedge. Retching.

Later, as Bella slept on the bunkbeds in Tad's old room, Wren and I sat on the sunporch watching storm clouds roll in from the West. We each had a glass of iced tea—sweet tea for Wren—and a small plate of cold chicken, sliced tomatoes off the vine, and a scoop of herbed potato salad I had made in the morning.

We talked lightly about our afternoon, and how much we both liked the Atwater house, and their beautiful view of the lake and sand dunes. I told Wren that I admired Lilian's taste in furniture, and enjoyed running my hands over the expensive upholstery.

"If I'm lucky, she'll redecorate in a few years," I said, referring to the like-new furniture I had purchased the year before. It now sat in the great room of the lodge, and in a handful of our cabins.

The sun room furniture Wren and I were sitting on was original to the lodge, but the cushions had been re-stuffed and re-upholstered the previous year.

"Or maybe she'll have to sell it all at an estate sale," Wren remarked quietly.

It took me a minute to realize what Wren was implying.

"Why would she have to do that?" I asked, trying to keep my voice conversational.

"I heard the valet talking to the bartender when I walked outside to ask for your Jeep," she said, after a pause. "They were saying they hoped to be paid in cash, because last time, the Atwater checks bounced."

Boom.

I didn't know a lot about teenagers, but I knew they were skittish. I tried to not overreact and scare Wren off. Because this was very interesting information.

"Hmm," is all I said, and then waited to see if there was more. There was—but not on the topic of the Atwater's finances.

"You seem to be feeling okay," I said.

Wren was quiet as she nodded, but didn't look at me.

"I'm glad the sun didn't make you sick today Wren."

"It wasn't the sun, Aunt Kay," Wren said very softly, "it was whatever Max and Bella were drinking from his little silver flask."

A shocking jolt ran through my body when she said that, and I jerked my head towards my young niece. Wren raised her eyebrows with intent, and nodded towards the apartment—I'm sure to warn me from waking Bella.

"Were they the only ones drinking?" I asked, barely whispering.

Wren took a moment to answer.

"No," she said at last. "Patti Lee took a sip or two. The other kids took more than a few. And I... I pretended because I felt pressured, but it was vile." Her chin quivered as she spoke.

And then, Wren leaned against my shoulder and broke into tears. "I miss Mama."

Oh, how I loved this sweet girl.

100

"I'm sure you do," I said. As I leaned my own head against the top of hers, I asked her, "What would your mama say, Wren?"

Wren sniffed and said, "She'd say, *be true to yourself, little bird.*"

Of course.

I felt a new respect for Selby just then. She had been so young when the girls came along. She had to raise them in the absence of Tad, certainly, who had been finishing up medical school and his residency. Selby had no doubt borne the brunt of illnesses, temper tantrums, potty training and teacher conferences—all by her *lil' ol' self.*

She and Tad both worked hard for his career, I realized just then.

I was glad she was enjoying an extended vacation, and I silently vowed to do a better job of keeping the girls safe until they returned. Even if I didn't achieve my goal of being their new best friend.

I must keep Selby's little birds safe in their summer nest.

28

I'm now fluent in "S'mores code"
-KERBY LODGE GUEST BOOK-

Loons, teens, and trees.

My thoughts overlapped and overwhelmed me as I tried to sleep the following morning.

Eventually, I got up and went to enjoy a quiet spell in the great room before any guests or girls awoke. If I was lucky, I could get in a cup of coffee and watch the loons gliding through the lake mist before it evaporated in the rising sun.

Loons are territorial, and smaller lakes might only have a single pair.

In a body of water the size of Lake Michigan, there are many loons— but they are rarely together. Except in the very early hours when they rendezvous, to socialize and bond with each other. Together, they prepare for their migration, I have read, and they possibly hammer out next season's mating plans, as they don't mate for life.

No one knows for sure.

The loons swim uneasily in a square-shaped pattern, until they disband. They need each other, that much is certain, but can only stand to be around each other for a short while.

Much like the tourists and the locals.

Bella and Wren had been at the lodge for nearly two weeks now. I was finally starting to feel like my old self, I realized, sipping my coffee. My trip to Europe with Luke seemed like a distant memory.

It must have been fading for Luke as well, because he was already thinking about the next trip. When we talked the night before, he enthusiastically shared his thoughts.

"We should go to New Zealand next July," Luke said, excitedly. "We can take an alpine wilderness hike, stay in castles, and cruise the fiords. Let's start planning it when I get back."

"Whoa, cowboy," I said, "I'm still recovering from Europe." "Recovering—you make it sound like the flu, instead of the great trip it was," he said.

He had an edge in his voice that made me pause.

"It was a great trip," I said, cautiously, "but I am still recovering from the jet lag, more than I expected. Remember, you're a seasoned traveler Luke—I'm sure I'll get used to it."

"Get used to it? I thought traveling was something we both wanted to do."

I could not seem to say anything right.

"It is. It is," I said. "Luke, honey, you can't see my face, and I can't see yours. I'm actually smiling at the thought of our next trip!"

I was not smiling at the thought of our next trip.

"So, let's shelve this until you return," I continued. "I just have a lot on my mind right now and I've got one foot in bed."

"That's fair," he said, "get some sleep and we'll talk tomorrow."

The honeymoon was over—I had officially lied to my husband.

About New Zealand.

"How was the Atwater party, Kay?" Hollis asked. Wandering into the dining room after the loons retreated, I got a fresh cup of coffee and sat down to talk with my intern.

"Weird," I said. "Opulent. Unsettling. Interesting."

"Wow," she said. "That's a lot of adjectives."

I smiled at her comment. "Did I miss anything?" I asked, and reminded her that the girls and I would be gone again this afternoon. The Wildberry lake party would hopefully be the polar opposite of all the drama and the posturing from the day before.

Hollis gazed around the room, and then looked at me rather pointedly. "Little Cody Gray spent most of the day here in the lodge, while his parents were nowhere to be seen. The little guy was despondent that he couldn't find Wren, and stuck to me like glue in her absence."

This was getting to be a problem. I'd avoided it so far because the Grays were guests, and I hadn't faced this problem before. Again, I wondered what Raya would do—had she encountered deadbeat parents?

I didn't want this family to feel unwelcome. I also feared getting a bad review on one of the many ratings websites that were so prevalent online. It was bad enough that opposing businesses often engineered bad reviews of their competitors—but to get an authentic bad review could torpedo all our efforts.

And with Stuart Gray sitting for hours on end on the deck, scrolling through his tablet, he could place a bad review of the lodge in the blink of an eye. For all I knew, that's what he did all day long—watch my staff for mistakes.

Cleaning crew short-sheeted our bed.
Light bulb flickers in the bathroom.
It rained on Tuesday, and their weather board said sun.

"I'll keep my eye on that," I promised. "It's certainly not your job to babysit, or Wren's. I've never seen anything like this—the families at Kerby Lodge have historically done everything together. That's what being here is all about!"

Hollis nodded, and reminded me that she would be away this afternoon as well. Knowing I couldn't cover for her, she had asked if her mother could come run the desk.

"She'll be happy for something new to do," Hollis said, "She's a little at odd ends over my brother and I being away at school, and Dad being occupied with his own retirement hobbies. Fishing, and golfing and stuff."

I thought that sounded great, and so Alice Fanning would be arriving shortly. To be honest, I'd agreed out of curiosity as much as anything. Who had raised this interesting young woman? I wanted to know. But I hoped poor old Alice wouldn't be ruffled by a clinging, demanding young Cody.

Taking my hot mug of coffee, I made my way outside to the carriage house. Jennifer was just opening her doors, and plugging in the coffee urn. As I sat down in a spare folding chair to catch up, an SUV came quietly down the road and parked.

"Your first customer already Jen," I said.

But I was wrong. It was Sue Spondike. "Can I join you two?"

Jennifer pulled up another folding chair so that the three of us formed a little half circle near the cash register. She poured a cup of coffee for Sue and handed it to her, and we all sat down. As customers arrived, Jen called out to let her know if they needed anything.

"Well this is fun," Sue said, "a mini class reunion."

We all smiled and agreed.

"Jennifer, I've been meaning to come see your shop," Sue was saying, "and running into Kay last night seemed like a good reminder."

I felt there was more to her visit, but waited for it to unfold.

104

I didn't have to wait long.

"Patti Lee was drinking last night at the Atwater's," she blurted out so that only we three could hear. "She said Max had a flask, and that everybody took sips—gulps—whatever."

"That's what I heard, too," I said.

"Jennifer," Sue said, "I'm sorry to skip the pleasantries this morning, and I know you see way too much of this. But Chip and I were shocked."

Jennifer nodded sympathetically and sadly it was true. As an EMT in a resort town, Jennifer, Patrick, and the other EMTs had to respond to unnecessary accidents as a result of people operating cars and watercraft under the influence. And the ages were skewing younger.

"Patti Lee, Bella and Wren, and Max... they're just kids," Sue said, shaking her head. "What were *we* doing at 16 and 17? My parents kept me so busy stocking and cleaning the gift shops, I didn't have time to get into trouble."

"Same here," I said, "I was folding sheets, picking up twigs that came down from the storms and wind, and pulling little sailboats in and out of the water."

"I always had two or three jobs going," Jennifer said.

We sipped our coffee and contemplated the seriousness of life for today's kids.

"I wanted Patti Lee to have more fun than I did in high school," Sue was saying, "but maybe my parents had the right idea."

Jennifer got up to help a customer, and Sue leaned over to me.

"The only reason I was there last night was because Skip Atwater is head of their association, and they are a big client of Chip's. But now, Skip wants Chip to invest in his failing business—and it almost feels like blackmail," Sue said, quietly. "Skip is going under fast since the recession, and he must be desperate to want *our* little pot of money."

Sue was underplaying their financial situation. It was well known that Chip "The Chipmunk," as Sue had once called him, had been squirrelling away money for a rainy day since he was a kid. He was frugal, and hard-working, and I trusted he was a wily investor—not one to throw good money after bad.

While Sue talked and went to refill her coffee, I discreetly pulled my phone out and sent Chip a text, reminding him about my trees. I slipped my phone back in my pocket.

"At dinner last night, Lilian was bragging about your sister-in-law's old money and your rich in-laws," Sue went on. "She inferred that you all would be investing in Skip's company, but that's how they operate. They make you think you're in good company."

This just confirmed that the Atwater's lived in a world I wanted nothing to do with, and I wondered how I'd gotten drawn in.

And how could I get out?

Just then, a Prius pulled up to the lodge and parked. A blonde-haired woman practically bounced out of the car, holding a tote bag. After smiling at our group, she looked over to Cody Gray, who had been circling the driveway on a plastic bike, looking bored and forlorn.

"You must be Cody," she said, "you can call me Alice. And if you run out of things to do today, I just might have what you're looking for in this bag."

To that, Cody's eyes grew wide as saucers.

The Pied Piper had arrived at Kerby Lodge.

29

Four out of five great lakes
Wish they were Lake Michigan.
-KERBY LODGE GUEST BOOK-

"I don't feel well," Bella moaned, "I'll be okay staying home alone."

I had just knocked on the girls' door to give them a two-hour warning before leaving for the Wildberry party. By now, I knew they'd grouse and procrastinate for at least an hour before even starting to get ready.

I had just enough time to lay down for a quick rest before getting ready myself. My salad was chilling in the refrigerator, and Alice Fanning was getting the lay of the land.

"I'm sure you'd be okay Bella, but I want you to come," I said in a no-nonsense voice that sounded surprisingly... parental. "You'll feel better after a long shower—or better yet, take a bath in Lake Michigan."

I heard her groaning, but it seemed to be one of defeat. Which was good. I myself might opt for a lake bath instead of a shower after my nap. There was nothing in the world as refreshing as taking a bar of peppermint soap out into the clear lake and lathering up.

Once, a guest tried to make me feel guilty, as if I were polluting the water. I gently reminded him that he himself had spent the day driving a boat powered by diesel fuel and oil; that he came over from Wisconsin on a ferry that dumps four tons of coal ash into the lake—daily; and that there was, most likely, a child peeing somewhere along the coastline.

"My little thimble-full of biodegradable soap in this ocean-sized lake is the least of our worries," I said.

Propping up my pillows and stretching out on my bed, I enjoyed the breeze from the lake blowing the curtains in. I thought about what Sue had said about the Atwater's—and wondered how the Kerby's had gotten mixed up with this family of ne'er-do-wells.

Could we keep our distance over the next two weeks until the girls went home? Not if Max persisted in wanting to be with Bella—there would no doubt be a confrontation between he and I, and maybe Lilian and I. And most likely Bella and I.

If Bella finds out that I knew she was drinking with Max on the jet skis, she might trace it back to Wren—and then I could lose Wren's trust. I had dug a deep hole by trying to make the girls happy. Which is the only reason I went last night.

One thing was clear, I had to keep Bella from returning to the Atwater's cottage.

But did Lilian really think we were friends? Would Skip invite Luke to his golf outings when he returned, and press him to invest in a failing business? Would the Atwater's reach out to my in-laws and ask them for money—suggesting that I was complicit?

My head was spinning. I was surely breaking all the rules that rich people live by.

And honestly, I felt sorry for the financial troubles of the Atwater family. I had nearly lost the lodge myself a few years back, and I wouldn't wish that on anybody.

Thankfully, Daniel Mayne swooped into my world. Though unwelcomed at the time, he made me see that the old ways my parents had put their trust in just weren't cutting it for a new generation of guests.

But unlike the Atwater family, I was never pretending to be something I'm not. From what I see, theirs is a house of cards—a life based on connections and appearances. The money they need to maintain this façade must be significant.

Yet, if the cards all tumble down around them, they'll be in good company.

The recession that slammed into us three or four years ago has been a great equalizer, upsetting the long-held beliefs that the rich would only get richer, and the locals in town would stick around and take care of them. But many businesses have imploded, and some people, like Skip, no longer have the money they once did.

By the same toss of the coin, new opportunities have arisen for people stuck in a "service" groove for generations. In the case of Mitch, the internet has provided a secondary income stream that has surpassed the

108

first. He could close his restaurant doors and be just fine. In fact, I hear he has a buyout offer from a national bakery brand. Contrary to most rumors I hear, I fervently hope this one is true.

Our local kids—once limited by a lack of proximity to large cities—have more options than ever. A few young people in our community have taken advantage of startup funds and launched lucrative businesses, further blurring the lines between the *haves* and the *have nots*.

The Skip Atwater's of the world may find that the local waitress at the yacht club is now the CEO of a tech startup. The boy who once loaded groceries in Lilian's car might be earning six figures selling mortgages from a remote office.

The biggest deals, once sealed on the golf course, now also take place in kayaks on the crystal summer rivers, and on snowshoes while traversing the winter dunes. The *de rigueur* of Lake Michigan millionaires used to be the Oxford shirt, but could now be a moisture-wicking pullover woven from bamboo fibers.

With time and tide waiting for no man, the world Skip knew like the back of his hand has turned upside down.

30

To the person who watched me dance on the beach like nobody was watching, Please erase the video from your phone.
-KERBY LODGE GUEST BOOK-

"Hey!" Jack and Stace found us immediately, and grabbed Wren and Bella by the hand to introduce them to their friends. Bella was finding it hard to maintain the sour expression she deliberately wore on her face.

Her displeasure was for my benefit, I was sure. She genuinely liked the twins.

The waterfront camp of Gramps Wildberry was a cleansing breath of fresh, authentic air, on the heels of my artificial evening at the presumptuous Atwater's.

After slowly ambling the Jeep down an unpaved rutted driveway, marked at the main road by a birchbark sign, the girls and I parked in a wooded clearing, without the help of a valet. Other cars were tucked under the heavy shade of the massive pines and oaks.

The girls and I made our way to the front of the ancient log and wood house with the battenboard shutters, and were greeted by a lively group.

"Kay, hello," I heard a voice behind me. "I guess we had the same plans today," Hollis surprised me. She had a relaxed smile on her face, and looked pretty in her cropped jeans and linen shirt. I noticed she wore a pale shade of lipstick, and had a natural glow about her.

Jack had invited her, she told me. They met at the lodge a few weeks ago, when the young designer came in as the bearer of bad news about the leak at Gram's house.

"We've hung out a few times," she said, blushing slightly, then turned to go catch up with the younger crowd. But not before pointing me in the direction of the kitchen.

I thought I should take my salad indoors and stick it in the refrigerator before going to meet Gramps. I didn't want the fresh basil to wilt. Letting myself in, I breathed in the scent of old wood and enjoyed the rugged décor. It was like walking through a well-edited antique store, where the very air carried the sweet aroma of history.

The house was dark, and ten degrees cooler than the outside air, which was to be expected. The old windows were small, the paneling was dark, and the trees that surrounded the property were dense.

There was an ancient upright piano next to a fieldstone fireplace; a vase of wildflowers sat on the hearth. On the ship-lapped walls, oval frames held sepia-toned photos of long-lost relatives—one portrayed a gathering on this very shoreline, from sixty or seventy years ago. A birch-bark framed photo depicted a wedding couple. Gramps and his bride, most likely.

His furnishings were well worn, but sturdy and inviting. A sofa upholstered in denim twill, accented with chairs covered in buffalo plaids. Feather down throw pillows were slip-covered in vintage chenille's and sturdy flour-sack cottons.

All Beth's touches, I was sure.

I heard Beth Wildberry before I saw her. She was laughing and joking with a man I couldn't see in the shadows of the kitchen doorway, but who had a deep laugh. Finally, I thought, I get to meet Beth's husband, who no one ever said boo about.

As I was about to enter the kitchen, I saw the backside of Beth as she leaned into an affectionate embrace from… Daniel Mayne.

"Uh…" I managed to say, as the three of us registered the unexpected presence of each other in the small space. We stood frozen for what seemed like minutes, all with the same suspended expression.

"Fridge?" I finally said, indicating the salad and breaking the spell.

Unruffled, Beth merely smiled and unwrapped Daniel's arms from her waist, saying "I'd better go check on Dad. I'm glad you're here, Kay."

I nodded as she went outside, finding it hard to take my eyes off my brother-in-law.

"Kay… Ker…" Daniel said my name slowly and deliberately, as if stalling for time.

As always, I could take a lesson from those who weighed and measured their words. Instead of having to do damage control, after saying things like: "Congratulations Daniel. A new love interest, complete with a set of twins."

Which I did say.

"That's a little catty Kay," Daniel replied, "and not like you."

Since returning from Europe, I had felt edgy and exhausted. But it was a poor excuse for bad manners.

"I'm… surprised, that's all," I said. But I wasn't being completely honest with Daniel, and he probably knew that. I was also aghast, and shocked.

"Surprised at what?" Daniel asked.

"Well…" I fumbled, "I thought you were in a committed relationship. And here you are, kissing the mother of our decorators. In the corner of a dark kitchen."

A slow smile spread on Daniel's face as I talked, but I couldn't tell him how hurt I felt.

Hurt that Jack and Stace had seen Daniel more than me. Had known what he'd been up to, when I didn't. Of course, the story of Daniel and Beth wasn't theirs to tell—it was his.

Mainly, I felt left out of the loop. And the realization that the *loop* wasn't mine to be in or out of was a bitter pill to swallow.

"No Daniel, I really am sorry for my words," I said again, sincerely, "forgive me."

He sized up my apology while I waited.

"Let me get you a cold Coke," he said, steering me outside. "Have you eaten today?"

I exhaled with relief at his kind demeanor.

Who could resist falling in love with tall, dark and handsome Daniel Mayne—besides me, that is? His brooding never suited me, especially once his cheerier younger brother began wooing my long dormant heart. But this man was a catch.

He was thoughtful and smart and loyal.

And that wasn't brooding I saw a few minutes ago when I walked in— I shook my head to erase the image of his strong tanned arms wrapped around Beth. In the shadows, he could have easily been my own husband.

Back outside, we sat down under an old oak, and looked out at the water. Bella and Wren, along with Jack, Stace, Hollis, and about four others were canoeing peacefully along the shore—talking to each other agreeably in words we could not make out.

Now, this was the unspoiled Lake Michigan I wanted to girls to know— the *Michigami*. Which was the original Ojibwa Indian word for Lake Michigan. It meant large lake. Large enough to hold our joys and carry away our troubles.

Powerful enough to obliterate a drop of organic peppermint soap.

I felt better after sipping my drink, and nibbling on a few crackers with spinach dip. After Daniel brought me the small plate, he told me that he and Francine had parted ways long ago. She is still a lifestyle blogger, but it wasn't Daniel's lifestyle she wanted.

"She's in California, working for a magazine," he said.

"Did you break your heart?" I asked, concerned for him. I had helped him pick up broken pieces before.

"No," Daniel said, turning his gaze to where Beth was standing. "Francine and I could never regain our footing after being apart for so long. And I think she sensed my heart was heading towards... in another direction."

Then he told me how he was drawn back to Beth Wildberry.

At first, their paths crossed because of his work with her twins. Then they discovered a shared interest in many things—design, art, architecture and food—so they began visiting galleries, and trying new restaurants.

I thought back to the time we visited an art gallery on a cold winter day, and how he came alive gazing at the expressions of paint and textiles.

Then a thought crossed my mind—had Daniel broken Francine's heart?

He must have anticipated this. "We parted amicably. No hearts were broken. No one was injured in the making of my relationship with Beth," he said, assuring me, and then smiled so broadly that I knew he must be in love. Maybe for the first time in his life.

"It was a clean break, and a fresh start," he said.

Daniel gave me the condensed version of Beth's story. She raised Jack and Stace as a young single mother after her divorce from their father. Before Beth's mother passed away, both of her parents had stepped in to fill the gap often left by her ex.

Beth shared Daniel's generation, sensibilities, and work ethic. She built a successful business from the ground up, and put her children through private schools and top universities, all while setting up her own retirement.

Beth Wildberry was not after Mayne money.

Taking a new look at Beth, who was laughing with her dad, I could see that she was really lovely in a way that confident, secure women tend to be—women who are sure of who they are, and of their place in the world. A place of their own making.

She would be a good partner for Daniel, I realized, and felt at peace.

But who could not be at peace while being on the Wildberry property— the cabin that time forgot? With the cars parked in the back, and no motors to be seen or heard for miles, the setting could easily be from a hundred years ago. There were only canoes and kayaks and rowboats gliding silently in the water—and guests on the shore sitting lazily on split log benches, swings suspended from tree branches, and on quilts spread out on the shaded grass.

Music came from an acoustic mandolin, and somebody began stacking logs on a stone-ringed firepit in anticipation of an extended evening watching the sun set.

And at that, I got up to go introduce myself to the man I suddenly admired so much. The man who created and preserved a true north woods *Eden* in a land of too many concrete developments, terraced condominiums, and flamingo-rampant associations.

"Daniel," I said, brushing the cracker crumbs off my lap, "it's good catching up and all, but I really came to meet Gramps."

31

You can't buy happiness, but if you're lucky,
You can buy a week at Kerby Lodge in the summer.
-KERBY LODGE GUEST BOOK-

"These toy cars were my son's, Cody," I overheard Alice saying as I entered the great room a few days later. She was sitting on the floor with him, in a corner by the book cases. The child was making *vroom vroom* sounds as he pushed them back and forth. "Pretend this whole room is a city, and drive them wherever you want."

The boy smiled up at her.

He could certainly monopolize the great room of Kerby Lodge all he liked on a sunny peak season day. It was hardly used except by guests passing through to the coffee pot, book shelves, and the makeshift lodge office. It wouldn't be fully occupied until mid-September, when guests started gravitating to the fireplace and reading nooks.

"In a little while, we'll get a snack," Alice said, getting up and walking to the desk.

August was flying by.

In another ten days, my brother and Selby would be arriving for a brief visit before taking the girls home. Nan and Sperry would be coming in for Labor Day weekend, they had confirmed. I hoped we'd be joined by June and Zeke, who hadn't committed.

Luke would be home in a few days—it felt like he'd been gone forever.

Hollis left to register for classes. She'd be in and out now, but her time with me was about to end. The silver lining could be summed up in two words: Alice Fanning.

Wiry and athletic, Alice seemed to have boundless energy. I wanted to be like her when I was in my fifties, but had to admit I wasn't much like her now, in my thirties.

"Alice, you're amazing," I said as I poured a cup of coffee from the urn. "I hope Cody isn't wearing you out." I had hoped Joy and Stuart would become more involved with the boy but it hadn't happened—and I dropped the ball on speaking to them.

But instead of feeling put-upon, Alice embraced the challenge. She brought different toys from her grown son's arsenal each day, and almost made a pre-school out of it.

Each morning, she had Cody help her draw the day's weather forecast on the white board in bright markers. He helped her measure the coffee grounds for the urn. They went outside and gathered different leaves from the trees, and then looked them up in a reference book from the great room shelves.

I could begin to see how Hollis had become the confident person she is.

Joy Gray even started sending a sack lunch for Cody when he arrived in the morning, then she'd come gather him up in the afternoon for his nap.

Alice was a force to be reckoned with, Stuart and Joy soon found out. The first time Cody came back to the lodge after his nap, she said, "Cody I'm so glad to see you, but this is *family time* and you must go find your daddy and mama and tell them so."

She told the boy that if his parents didn't believe him, to send them to her.

"*I'll* tell them," Alice said in no uncertain terms, with a smile on her face.

That's all it took. Cody belonged to Alice from morning through lunch time, and Joy and Stuart seemed to rally enough to parent the boy after his nap.

"We just don't know what's going on, Kay," Alice told me, shaking her head. "Let's give this little guy a good vacation, and let his folks figure things out."

I nodded, but was indignant and a little angry with this couple for their negligence. It wasn't lost on me that I was doing the same thing with Bella and Wren—today, anyway. They were off to spend the day with Sue Spondike and Patti Lee.

Sue called to invite the girls to a merchandising show in Traverse City. She would be ordering her inventory for the next year, and wanted the teens' input. "They'll get a lot of free goodies," Sue said, "and we will eat like kings all day."

The girls jumped at the chance, though I overheard Bella placating somebody on her phone—could it be Max? "I *know*," she said in a loud whisper, "I wanted to hang out with you too. Maybe tonight, if I get home in time."

Fat chance, I thought.

I hadn't seen Max since his mother's party, and didn't realize he and Bella had been talking. That was naïve on my part.

"Don't hurry back," I said to Sue, and meant it.

All the situations that had been troubling me during the past few weeks were inevitably either coming to a close, or to a head, yet I hadn't resolved any of them.

I hadn't managed the problem with Cody, and his inattentive parents.

I hadn't talked to Luke about our uncomfortable conversation, regarding our expectations of each other. "You're not Fitz," I had said in anger, levelling that at him like an insult. What was that?

I hadn't evicted Daniel from the A-Frame, or given him any warning.

Gram's house was nowhere near ready to move into.

As for my nieces, I was no closer to being their friend than when they came. Oh, I'd had a moment with Wren, and Bella had put her claws away for the most part. But would we be family before they left—and not just distant relations?

One afternoon, I tried to bridge the gap between us by pulling out one of the boxes from Gram's house that was being stored in the apartment. It contained hundreds of old photos of myself, Tad, June and Zeke, Fitz and Raya, and Gram—how fun it would be to draw the girls out by asking them to sort these with me.

Maybe they could begin to get a sense of the history of Kerby Lodge, and finally see that this place is their heritage, and not their prison.

"What is this, Aunt Kay," Bella had sneered, "our camp craft? Do you want us to glue popsicle sticks on these and put on a puppet show? Maybe we can weave potholders next."

Defeated, I silently closed the box and put it behind a chair in the great room.

Max and Lilian were another problem. Somehow, I had given them the impression that I was a willing pawn in whatever game they were playing. I imagined Lilian out there telling stories about my family's finances, and worse—saying we were investors in Skipper's schemes. This alone was enough to make me angry.

I was also angry about Max and Bella and their underage drinking a few days ago at the Atwater's—angry at Lilian for condoning it. Angry that Max pressured Wren and the others. Angry at Bella for succumbing. And I was angry at myself for not dealing with any of it.

Suddenly, more than anything, I wanted to be back at the Wildberry camp—the most pure, unspoiled spot on Lake Michigan. I think that's how Kerby Lodge must have seemed forty-some years ago when my parents bought it.

Before the guests began arriving.

Before the brochures, and the jet skis, and the website, and the renovations, and the cars zipping in and out, Kerby Lodge was a few old rocking chairs on an ancient front porch.

And silence.

The loudest noise at the Wildberry log house was the closing of the screen door. Which was a comforting, nostalgic sound.

"Kay, I like to hear the loons and the wind," Gramps Wildberry told me. "I prefer smelling my coffee, rather than boat engines," he said. "I'm too old to change my ways."

I just nodded, and really listened.

We sat side by side on a double glider, rocking back and forth and gazing at the water. In the absence of gadgets and electricity, we could hear people talking, and a fire crackling. Nobody looked at their phones. It was as if modern technology didn't exist at this sanctuary.

"Your dad was the same as me," he said, surprising me. "Oh yeah, I knew him; your dad was a fine fellow and a good friend to the community. Stood up for what he believed in. He loved the early morning woods, and the wildlife. He developed his land, but he also *preserved*."

Gramps was right. Fitz Kerby was a preservationist at heart. He kept the shoreline and the lodge as it was wherever possible, and used materials at hand. The hand-hewn stairs in the A-Frame, for instance, were from a fallen tree.

I had altered and changed the lodge beyond recognition in many ways. Though I could argue that revealing the heart pine floors was more restoration than renovation. But it couldn't be helped. Kerby Lodge was too vast and costly to be treated as my private rustic home. I had to appeal to my audience, or lose the place altogether.

"These new developers have a different way of thinking," Gramps told me. "They advertise *Come Live in the North Woods,* then they bulldoze all the trees and vegetation. They destroy all the habitats and ecosystems," he said.

"The buyers come to the woods, and want to see a little bit of wildlife, but only on their terms. They see these little animals skittering around, Kay—looking for their homes—and by golly, they call the DNR to come get rid of them," he chuckled and shook his head.

Interrupting our conversation was a twig breaking in the woods. We both turned to see a buck and a doe eating berries in the brush—a late summer feast, compliments of the Wildberry family. After a few nibbles, the pair darted off again into the thick forest.

I nodded in agreement as I listened to Gramps, but had more than a twinge of regret about taking out the pine trees, and the many habitats the grove represented, just to give delicate little brides a bit of manufactured shelter from the elements. If they couldn't take a little rain, then maybe they shouldn't be getting married to begin with.

Maybe I needed to sit these brides down and tell them about problematic days, and multiple crock pots. About stacks of boxes and leaky pipes. About long-distance phone calls that end in lies and deception about wanting to visit New Zealand.

About wanting to get off the phone just so you can go eat cookies in bed.

"Toughen up, buttercup," is what I'd tell a bride if it was raining on her wedding day at Kerby Lodge. "A little rain is going to fall sometime—why not today?"

The realization that I would be the worst wedding consultant ever was probably reason enough to reconsider my destination wedding dreams. I almost wished I hadn't sent Chip another text this morning, pushing him to commit to a tree removal date. His response times were slowing down considerably, I noticed.

And his icons weren't quite as friendly.

32

After a week here, my B.P. is so low,
I think I may be in a coma.
-KERBY LODGE GUEST BOOK-

"Lilian Atwater is a bag of wind."

There was no sleep in Nan's voice when I picked the phone up off my bedside table and mumbled *hello*. It was early morning and still murky outside as she launched her monologue.

"I will not be going to her yacht club Labor Day weekend—as she has been gossiping all over Chicago," she said.

I was so relieved to hear her say this. Apparently, tales of Lilian and Skip's investor woes had reached their Chicago acquaintances, and Nan was hopping mad over having her own good name associated with this opportunistic family.

"She bought a bracelet five years ago," Nan said. "We are not—I repeat, not friends. And we are not investors in whatever scheme they've cooked up. I will tell her myself."

As Nan talked and I listened, I wandered up the Kerby Lodge road towards the tennis court. I didn't want to lose my phone reception, especially while Nan was on a tear. Or wake the girls, who would be asleep for hours still. As would most of our guests.

Nan and I were morning people. It was a necessity of business ownership, but it was also our natures.

After she arrived for our wedding reception last September, she and I nearly bumped into each other in the darkened great room before the following sunrise, both stumbling to the coffee urn. Subsequently, we enjoyed watching the morning light together from the sun room as we quietly became better acquainted.

She was so much like Daniel in this regard. While Luke makes his appearance at a respectable morning hour, I will never beat Daniel or Nan in a "rise and shine" contest. Walking up the road in the growing light of dawn, I thought of our coffee klatches last summer, and looked forward to her Labor Day visit even more.

Thankful for the warm Kerby Lodge sweatshirt I had thrown on, I breathed in the fresh, cold air. The colors hadn't started turning just yet, but the deep greens of summer were dormant, and fading into golds. Russet tips were showing on some of the shrubs. And the perennial flowers were saying their final farewells in anticipation of the first frost.

Walking past cabins and cottages, I quietly murmured "mm hm" as Nan spoke.

When Nan had finished ranting about Lilian, she asked me how my summer was going. There was something in the tone of her voice. It transitioned from her usual Boston-accented no-nonsense clip into the warm concern I was used to hearing from Luke, and even Daniel.

It caught me by surprise, and the floodgates opened.

As I sat on the bench next to the tennis courts, I told her about the girls, the Atwaters, and the stalled renovations. I whined about how some days the jet lag seemed worse, and not better; and even about little Cody Gray.

I whined about Luke being gone.

As I rambled on, I told myself to *stop*, and not overwhelm this poor woman. Or make her wonder why her good son had married such an incompetent person. But it all spilled out like water, until I was empty.

I could only wait and see what damage I had done.

"Kakah," she said at last, and I held my breath, "thank you."

Thank you?

"Thank you, sweet girl," she went on, "for confiding in me. Talking to me as a friend."

Somehow, I had made Nan happy. This good woman who had worked so hard to raise her sons to be strong, confident men, only to have them leave her nest to wander in the wilderness. Leaving her to bury herself in work, and charities—with the hope that someday she would have daughters-in-law who did not despise her.

"You will, no doubt, solve everything," Nan said, sounding confident it would be so. "And someday dear, you will look back on this *summah* as one of the best of your life."

"Nan... I love you," I said, quietly sniffling.

There was a pause, and I wondered if she heard me.

"I love you too, Kakah," she said.

One of the best *summahs* of my life—that seemed so unlikely. Was that in my control? There wasn't much summer left. And aside from our trip, it was the absolute worst.

I gazed over at Gram's house, dark and quiet as it was, and my heart sank. Last year at this time, Luke and I were settling into that house and getting ready for a new life, and new jobs. There was so much excitement; so many possibilities ahead for us.

But now, Luke would be coming home once again to the overcrowded apartment. I thought about this as I sat, feeling like a failure.

A wave of guilt hit me as strong as a Lake Michigan undertow.

Luke had grown up in a comfortable home. As an adult, he lived in cozy well-appointed apartments as he moved from one location to the next with his teaching career. And now, I had him living out of a suitcase, in an overcrowded postage stamp of a bedroom. Where he had to navigate packing boxes to get to my too-small childhood bed.

The man signed on for me, not Kerby Lodge, with all its quirks and eccentricities. I was enough of a *quirk*—he certainly didn't need to live in a junky museum, as Bella called the apartment, to prove his love for me.

I thought about all he'd given up—a chance to live overseas, or in Alaska; a chance to see the world. He could be anywhere doing anything, and I could be with him. We could have gone together. Why did I make it seem as though Kerby Lodge and I were a package deal?

Poor, sweet man.

Luke has proven his love over and over again, and what sacrifices have I made? Not one, unless going on a dream vacation counted as a sacrifice.

I endured a trip to Europe.

He deserved far better. If I only solved one of my summer dilemmas, I decided, then let it be the renovation on the house. I didn't care whose feathers I would ruffle, or whose party I would poop, I was going to light a fire under our contractors and get them back to work.

My husband deserved a home to come home to.

Still sitting on the bench, I watched the last of the cold mist dissipate down towards the lake. The windows of the lodge were backlit and dark. Behind me, cars traveled on the main road into town. Some drove out of town towards the larger cities.

As the sun got higher, the woods began filling with light, sending the little animals into hiding again until tonight's inky dusk. I took a deep breath of cool August air, and could smell the sharp notes of late summer, and the encroaching autumn.

September was around the corner—there was no denying it. There was only a little while left to make this one of the best summers of my life, and not a total disaster.

And just then, to my amazement, one of the vehicles on the main road stopped and turned onto the Kerby Lodge road—it was a work truck. It passed me, and traveled all the way down, beyond the lodge. I could see by its tail lights that it parked at the A-Frame.

Before I could even smile, or *hoot*, which I wanted to do, another two work trucks turned onto my road, then veered into the driveway of Gram's house.

I grinned like it was Christmas morning, seeing four men exit the trucks, holding their coffee cups and unloading their ladders and tool boxes. Right behind them, in a restored 1967 El Camino, came the twins. Stace dropped off Jack, and then continued down the lodge road, presumably to give marching orders at the A-Frame.

It wasn't yet 8 a.m., but this morning was off to a remarkable start, I thought, happily. And then came the cherry on the top. Alice Fanning drove past me and gave me a little wave from her virtually silent Prius. She was on her way to make coffee, welcome early morning guests, and make one little boy and his parents very happy.

I stood up and began walking down the road with a spring in my step.

Best summah ever.

33

I read a book. A whole book.
And nothing but the book.
-KERBY LODGE GUEST BOOK-

"*Mornin'* Luke. Just wanted you to know that your mama is going to drive here in her Land Rover and kick Lilian Atwater's bee-hind. Love you."

This was the message I left on my husband's voicemail as I walked away from the tennis court bench. Though it was very early, he called right back. I walked a few feet into the woods and sat down again—right on the cold rock where Luke found me over a year ago.

Miraculously, the call did not disconnect.

"Sheesh, Kaker, I've only been gone a few weeks. What's going on there?" He said.

And suddenly I was laughing so hard that I couldn't even talk, just picturing the look on his face—and imagining a face-off between Nan and Lilian. An hour ago, I had planned to tell him that everything here was falling apart. But now, I didn't think I'd sound convincing.

"I haven't met Lilian," Luke said sleepily as I laughed, "but my money is on Nan."

"Mine too," I managed. And then I said, "Luke I've missed you, and I've been feeling sorry for myself with you gone—that's not fair to you."

"I miss you too, Kaker Mayne," he said. "I can't wait to come home and be with you. Just you and me… and two teenaged girls… and a few hundred storage boxes… and lodge guests knocking on the apartment door, wearing ridiculous flannel PJ pants with polar bears on them. Looking for those little bars of soap."

And then we were both laughing.

"Two more days." I said, hanging up.

The unexpected happiness I felt that morning was quickly tested when I saw Max Atwater's FIAT pull into the lodge driveway, and simultaneously heard Bella entering the great room from the apartment.

I had to think fast—there was a wolf at the door.

"Max and I are going to his house, and then sailing, Aunt Kay," Bella was telling me, more than asking me.

Just then, Max walked in and eyed me warily, as I eyed him.

"Oh sorry, no," I said to them both, "I already made plans for just us girls."

Bella shot me an angry look. I'm sure she was wondering what lame plans I had for them this time—a twig craft?

Taking pound cake to shut-ins?

She opened her mouth to protest when I threw the biggest bucket of cold water on her wrath I could think of.

"Shopping!" I blurted out in the general vicinity of Max. "I'm taking the girls shopping in Petoskey for the day. They'll want new clothes for school. And shoes!"

Bella was immediately conflicted. As much as she wanted to spend the day with the intoxicating, rebellious young Max, the lure of new clothes was strong. I had to seal the deal.

"Bella," I said, "why don't you grab the keys for my SUV, and drive it around to the front. We'll take that today."

I would buy their love, as Luke had suggested. Or at the very least I would buy their safety for a day—safety from this rogue young man and his destructive tendencies. And from their own youth and impulsiveness.

Today I would protect Selby's little birds, and if I was lucky, move one step closer to knowing who they really are. Beyond my shallow Christmas card perceptions.

As Max steamed, Bella glided lithely to the key drawer and walked past him.

She shrugged at him as if to say "what can I do—it's shopping, Max, for new clothes. And I am 17!" She went to get the shining champagne-toned SUV from the garage.

After Bella left the room, I leveled my gaze at Max. "Best not to make plans with my nieces without checking with me first," I said, "I wouldn't want to inconvenience you. Again."

The smirk on his face was reminiscent of our encounter on Daniel's deck, but unlike that day, he couldn't hold it for long. Not against the steely resolve I wore on my own face.

His smirk may have been born of his entitled upbringing, and nurtured by the pressure he no doubt felt from his parents, but my resolve was grounded in the mighty Raya—deflector of the *cauld winds*. And of Fitz— fighter for what he believed in.

It was buoyed by the powerhouse Nan, disdainer of all things Atwater. The love of Luke, the righteousness of Daniel, and the *spit and vinegar* of Aunt June.

And finally, by the no-nonsense presence of Alice Fanning, who watched closely but discretely, and approvingly I think, from the dining room.

"Yes ma'am," Max said at last. Smoldering.

I was a loon, with a full wing span.

34

This vacation was a second place prize at an auction.
#shouldabeenfirstplace
-KERBY LODGE GUEST BOOK-

The wind was picking up.

I noted this as I drove back to the lodge later that evening, after a full day of shopping. The girls tried on and modeled hundreds of pieces for me and for each other.

"Love it." they said over and over.

Love it.

Love it!

My bank card was warm to the touch most of the day. It barely had time to cool down, as I pulled it out of my wallet time and time again.

Apparently, our backwater town, as Bella had once said, is very fashion forward.

I was proud of myself for never looking at a single price tag the entire day—the girls never did. My only thought was of that new hospital wing, and how it would just have to wait.

The car was silent as I drove.

Luke had said that teenagers are like toddlers, and if that's true, I am a success! I wore them out enough to sleep all the way home. Teens and toddlers, it seems, are happy when they get what they want. It wasn't sustainable, of course, but it made for a nice change of pace from the glowering and pouting—and I could see the appeal.

Sleepy myself, I grabbed a carryout coffee to sip as I traveled along the shoreline. Heavy winds buffeted the substantial side panels of the SUV, and I was glad not to be getting blown around in the little Jeep.

If these winds persist, there will be a red flag at all the beaches and marinas tomorrow. That flag tells swimmers to stay on the beach and don't enter the water. With a red flag flying, Max and Bella cannot possibly go sailing or swimming, or out on his jet ski.

Even the blustery Lilian and the forceful Max can't challenge the fetch of the wind.

People think they can "wade in" on such days, but quickly discover that the waves will batter their legs like high school wrestlers, knocking them over and pinning them down. And the waves aren't the only danger. The less visible currents can pull swimmers quietly into deep water and then under, out of sheer exhaustion. The scariest movie can't compete with the frightening power of the Great Lakes during inclement weather.

I realized this summer that teenagers aren't going to admit their vulnerability. They're like swimmers caught in a too-strong current who don't know they are in trouble until it's way too late. That's what warning flags are for, and lifeguards.

And parents. And aunts.

Max Atwater was a red flag, but Bella couldn't see it.

Bella and Wren were dazzling, and deceptively beautiful—just like the lake when the sun reflects off it, looking like millions of diamonds and crystals. When we were shopping, and they were happy, I could almost believe these girls were reasonable human beings who wouldn't cause a moment of anxiety. I almost let my guard down.

But if we forget the invisible under-currents even for a moment, we do so at our peril.

"How did you know you loved Uncle Luke," Wren asked me while we were enjoying a late lunch in downtown Petoskey. We had already stuffed the SUV full of shopping bags, and were ready to murder some sweet teas and whitefish sandwiches. Yes, we'll have fries with that—and pie, I told the waiter.

I stalled for a minute while I ate my lunch.

How did I know?

How does one fall in love over the phone?

I wanted to think long and hard before I answered, in light of the times we now live in. I don't pay too much attention to the goings-on of the world, but my head isn't completely in the sand. I understand that all over the world, women fall prey to online romances and virtual Romeos; to schemes that often result in broken hearts and empty bank accounts.

"I'm not sure," I said, in all honesty. "But I believe it's when I knew he really cared about me, and wanted what was best for me." I went on to say that Luke got to know me through Daniel's blog, and through our many conversations. We were acquaintances first, then friends.

"In every picture on the blog, I was wearing an old flannel shirt and holding a paint roller," I said, "so he certainly got a glimpse of the real, unpolished me."

But I needn't have worked so hard at choosing my words, trying to convince them that I wasn't vulnerable when I fell in love with Luke, because they had stopped listening. When, I didn't know. Probably when they realized how good the cell reception was in Petoskey.

I shrugged to myself and ate another bite of my sandwich.

"Why do you hate Max?" Bella surprised me then, as I took a drink of tea. Carefully, I set my glass down.

"Do you think I hate Max, Bella?" I turned the question around.

She looked at me and did the same, "Do you think we're too young?"

"Too young to date? No," I said, thinking about Sue and Chip, and even Tad and Selby, who fell in love in college. "Too young for drinking the way you two do? Yes."

Bella was quiet.

"Max could be a good man when he gets older, if he decides to be," I elaborated, not sure I believed my own words, "but right now his life is out of control and he doesn't know where to look for help."

Max drinks to push down the pressures he feels at home, I told Bella and Wren, though I admitted to not knowing why. Pressure to get good grades maybe, or scholarships? Pressure to pretend their family finances were sound?

From what I'd seen, there was enough pressure to go around in the Atwater household these days. They were a collective powder keg, about to explode.

But why was Bella drinking with him? Was she angry at me, or her parents still for removing her from Atlanta for the summer? Why is she so eager to be liked by Max and his friends—is alcohol the price of entry into his luxurious life? Her life is luxurious too.

I could only hope that she actually heard my words. There was no guarantee, I realized, feeling like every adult in the world talking to a teenager. But that didn't give me a pass on saying the hard things that needed to be said.

"He is drawn to your confidence and stability, Bella, because he's missing those qualities in his own life," I said. "But at the same time, he wants to destroy those qualities in you—because underneath his cute blonde hair, Max is…"

I scrambled for the right word.

Dangerous? Yes, but Bella is drawn to that quality.

Reckless? Again, she wants to dip her toe in *recklessness*—something she's never been allowed to do as a sheltered and protected daughter.

"Max is *selfish*," I said, "a trait that neither of your parents would approve of. He doesn't want anyone to have what he can't have."

Bella held my gaze, weighing and measuring my words against her own desire to break free this summer—from the restraints she has undoubtedly felt throughout her young life, until a *ding* from her phone broke the spell. An incoming text drew her eyes downward.

Max Atwater, no doubt.

35

Thank you for signing up with VeRoom.com,
It was an amazing and affordable spontaneous week.
-KERBY LODGE GUEST BOOK-

"How do you stop the wind, Luke?"

I was talking to my husband on the phone the following day, as he packed his bags to fly home the next day. On the water, there was a full fetch of the wind, blowing from the west side of Lake Michigan all the way to the shores of Kerby Lodge.

The waves crashed loudly, and the skies were overcast. It was not a good beach day, even just to soak up the sun. If I didn't know better, I'd swear it was the shoulder season, showing up early and unannounced.

Every Labor Day, I watched with interest as the weather changed, and the winds picked up. As a kid, I pictured it blowing the summer tourists back to their homes—back to Detroit, Chicago, and Minneapolis. Sweeping them out the door.

I smiled to think the Atwater's might go home early!

As the owner of the inn, however, my perspective changed. I wasn't always so eager to see peak season end. Especially if I didn't clear enough income to pay my growing tax bill, and keep the inn in good repair.

After hoisting the lodge's red flag to full mast, I sat in the kitchen of the little apartment with a cup of tea. I had allowed the girls to take my Jeep into town to meet Patti Lee and a few others for lunch. I checked with Sue to make sure she knew about it, and she did.

"Trust, but verify," Luke had said, in one of his tiresome lectures to me on teens.

"They will all be back in school in just over a week's time," Sue lamented, and she was right. Luke and I included.

Last year, I subbed for Rhonda Ellis while she was on maternity leave. This year, I would be a floating sub, filling in where needed. I wasn't disappointed. There were a handful of teachers in various grades who were about to retire, and I could get more of a sense of where I might fit in as a full-time teacher by sampling all their classes.

"The answer is, you can't," Luke was saying.

I had forgotten the question already.

"You can't stop the wind, Kaker," he went on, and then I remembered. "If you're talking about Bella and Wren and Max, and the forces of nature, you can't stop the wind. You can only batten down the hatches."

Luke was right. Even if the heavy winds subsided, I needed to be on guard. Max was always nearby, I was sure. He may even be in town with the girls this very minute.

And I was sure I hadn't heard the last of Lilian Atwater, either.

"Luke, honestly I don't know how Mum did it. How did she run the lodge and keep such a close eye on Tad and I when we were growing up? She seemed to always know where we were, and what we were up to," I said.

"Fitz was there too, right?" Luke said.

"Yes, that's my point," I countered. "I am drowning with these girls, and starting to realize that between our travel and your work, you won't be around during the peak seasons."

There were a few minutes of silence between us.

"Is that what you meant when you said I wasn't Fitz?" Luke asked.

"I don't know what I meant, Luke," I said with all honesty. "I was hurt and lashing out. You see, all my life I've compared myself to Raya and never felt I measured up."

"So, when I told you that you weren't your mother," he said, "it felt like an attack."

"I guess it did," I said.

"But what you said to me was true," Luke said, softly. I sensed he had stopped packing and was giving me his full attention. "I'm not your dad. I'm not an innkeeper, or a handyman… I am not any of those things that made Fitz Raya's perfect partner. I'm sorry that I'm falling short in your eyes."

I had such a lump in my throat that I could not speak.

36

Just as doctors can never get sick, and barbers can't have a bad hair day, innkeepers... well, innkeepers are supposed to create a perfect haven for their guests. Even when their own worlds are falling apart.

Fitz and Raya did this flawlessly—I was the one who couldn't keep my head in the game. As Luke pointed out, I spent twelve years hibernating after my parents died.

But what did people expect? I was devastated by their deaths, and fairly blindsided by the gift of the lodge. There was never a succession discussion with Fitz and Raya; never a suggestion that I might major in hotel management, or even take a few business classes. My parents didn't give me a single clue.

I just assumed that... what *did* I assume? For one thing, that my parents would never die so young, or so unexpectedly. That Tad should be the rightful heir, for another. Tad, the cheerful concierge of the rusty bikes.

But Tad couldn't leave home fast enough.

And did I really think he was going to give up his medical career? That he would trade fixing broken bones for a broken down lodge?

Maybe Fitz and Raya thought that over time, one of us would want the lodge, and the lifestyle. Maybe they tossed a coin before making their will, and I was the winner—or the loser.

As their reluctant successor, I bumped along, fumbling in the dark and making all kinds of mistakes. But now I was learning, one painful lesson after another. The most recent being the realization that people bring their problems to Kerby Lodge. Naively, for years I thought that each family that tumbled out of their Wagoneer or minivan was as happy as the next.

I saw things now. The stresses and the sadness. The attempts to cope. And I didn't like it. Not one bit. This was a carefree place, for fun and relaxation. But I could hardly screen guests for grief—it was not an unleashed pet, running wild.

It was not a restriction I could enforce.

No smoking.

No sorrows.

No drama.

We've probably had many troubled families at Kerby Lodge through the years, and I just never knew or noticed. But from the start, I did notice that the Gray family was troubled.

Joy Gray played with Cody a little bit, but left this boy to entertain himself for most of his days. Stuart Gray barely interacted with his wife and son. Instead, he chose to sit and read a book or look at his tablet all day long in the shade.

Several times, I came close to reprimanding them for their negligence—and for expecting us to be their babysitters. But there was never the right opportunity, so I said nothing. And now they were at the tail end of their stay.

The Gray family would be leaving in a few days, and I couldn't wait. They were a constant reminder to me that I still had a long way to go as an innkeeper. They foisted their little boy on my niece Wren, and then Alice Fanning, and I had allowed it.

I felt sorry for the little guy, and the life of absentee parenting he'd be going back to.

Thinking of these things, I walked back to the lodge from Gram's house, where to my great pleasure, the walls were being painted, and the new flooring was being installed. Luke and I would have to sleep at the innkeeper's apartment, but not for long.

Entering the lodge through the heavy front door, I heard low murmurs and sniffles. Someone was definitely crying! Was Bella all right?

But no, it wasn't Bella.

As I rounded the corner from the great room into the dining room, I could see Joy Gray sitting in a dining room chair, bent over and sobbing. She was being comforted by Alice, who had her hand resting lightly on Joy's back. Making a quick visual sweep of the room for Cody, I could see through the windows that Cody was on the beach with Stuart.

I was about to retreat, when Alice drew me in.

"Kay, Joy here was just telling me how grateful she is for Kerby Lodge, and the good care we've taken of them, and little Cody," Alice said in soothing tones, for Joy's benefit, no doubt.

Joy lifted her head and made eye contact with me. After drying her eyes, she sat up a little straighter and took a few deep breaths. I pulled out a chair and sat down.

"I know you think we are... terrible... parents," Joy said, gulping air.

Yes, I did think they were terrible parents, and wanted to say that. For once, however, I took a page from the stoic Mayne's and held my tongue.

This allowed Joy to go on.

"You see, we've had a... family tragedy," Joy continued. "A baby, born very ill..." and at that, Joy had a catch in her throat. Alice and I said nothing as Joy wrestled with her emotions until she could speak again.

"We miss her terribly, but we are healing," Joy said. "It's very fresh, you see, and every time poor Stuart looks at Cody, he sees her little eyes in his."

I swallowed hard.

"Stuart breaks down, and that upsets Cody, which is why he's kept his distance," she said. "But he's a good dad, and he loves Cody—we both do. We want to help him to heal, too. At the moment, we are just getting by. One day at a time."

"So you see," Joy continued, "you've given us a much-needed breather, and thanks to Alice," and at this, Joy did her best to smile up at the heartbroken, compassionate face of Alice Fanning, "we now feel we can work to find our new normal. As a family."

Alice had tears in her eyes, I could tell, through my own watery eyes.

Joy went on to tell Alice how her little routine had helped them see that structure would be good for the Gray family. When they got home, they would both take Cody to pre-school in the mornings, then have "family time" in the evenings. And eventually...

Alice nodded, signaling to Joy that no more needed to be said.

Joy dried her tears, and then walked through the great room and out the sunroom door, making her way down the path to the beach. Taking her aching arms and broken heart with her. I fervently hoped they would enjoy their last days together at Kerby Lodge.

I thought of all the ill will and bad opinions I had about the Gray family, that I wish I could take back now. Imagine if I had verbalized some of what I was thinking—how much more damage could I have caused this grieving family? I cringed at the thought.

Of course, if I had known all this before—but no. Guests may unpack their luggage when they arrive, but the baggage takes a while.

37

"Have you gone off *Irish Lace*, lad?"

Fresh from the emotional exchange with Joy Gray, I found myself in a face-off with Daniel Mayne over the color of the A-Frame walls. Standing nose to nose in the middle of the room, hands on our hips, we had a full peanut gallery watching us, including our decorators and painting crew, and the odd construction worker.

I had meant my words to be playful, but if the faces surrounding me were any indication, I missed the mark.

But when Jack and Stace mentioned that Daniel wanted to warm the tones of the A-Frame a little, I felt a fiery emotion well up inside of me befitting my red hair and Scottish heritage. Four gallons of paint sat on the floor, marked Greige Sky.

In spite of my indebtedness to him, Daniel's decision felt like a personal affront.

Did he really think the A-Frame was his own—that he had squatter's rights, simply because if it weren't for himself, none of us would have Kerby Lodge to call our home?

"Are you *playin'* favorites with this cabin, Daniel?" I asked him, the brogue unintentional, but there nonetheless.

"I'm not *playin'* favorites, Kay Kerby Mayne," Daniel was throwing the brogue back at me with a fairly respectable impression.

I tried not to smile as I fought to make my case.

I remembered the day in the paint store, when Daniel had picked Irish Lace out of the seemingly hundreds of whites on the menu. It touched my heart, knowing that my mum, Raya, had married my dad wearing Irish Lace.

The paint color felt like her blessing, and Daniel knew this.

I said in a throaty whisper, "Are you denying Raya's blessing to the A-Frame, Daniel," feeling my chin quiver, and my smile turning to tears that were about to spill as my emotions seemed to be having a field day.

"Kaker," Daniel said, concern on his face replacing any combativeness, playful or otherwise.

Nearby, Jack and Stace made a show of looking at paperwork. The painters had taken out their sandwiches, and were scrolling through their phones. One guy scratched his head and looked at his watch. I knew that if we didn't decide today, I could lose the painters for another week—maybe longer. I couldn't let that happen.

"In the lodge," Daniel said, "we painted the walls, and then we designed."

"Okay," I said, remembering.

"But we need to think of Nan's pieces, and work around those," he said. "That is, unless you want to re-cover the upholstery. At considerable expense."

He had me there. Someday I might need to re-cover them, after a few years of guests throwing their sandy towels over the arms of the furniture, or plopping down with sloshy mugs.

But for this one shining moment, the expensive Teal and Aspen textiles were in perfect condition. It was as if Nan had the pieces vacuum-packed and bubble wrapped, I told Luke, then stored in a climate-controlled room where they were never touched.

"Yeah, that's pretty much how it went down," Luke responded.

If I okayed the paint, it would all come together for Labor Day, and I could host Nan and Sperry in style. Everything would be beautiful and new for a hot minute—long enough for Nan to see how pretty everything looked, with her generous "cast-offs."

Just like old times, the Mayne's of Chicago would enjoy their stay at Kerby Lodge, complete with their son Daniel.

And Luke, if he so desired.

Though Daniel was waiting, I couldn't help but smile as I turned to look out towards the lake. My mind was wandering to a sweet memory from the night before, when I suggested to Luke that he might want to join his family in the A-Frame.

Last night, long after everyone else turned off their lamps and had gone to sleep, Luke surprised me by arriving home a half day sooner than expected.

"Luke!" I fairly yelled, and he held his finger to my lips so as not to wake anyone.

I flew into his arms for a warm and welcoming hug, and kisses—so many that I lost count. It was a nearly perfect homecoming, that I nearly ruined with my quick temper.

When Luke had cringed, only slightly, at having to maneuver around the boxes in the apartment again, I told him he was more than welcome to go stay in the A-Frame, along with his brother and his parents.

"Won't you boys have fun, camping on the floor in sleeping bags. Just like when you were kids," I suggested. "You two can..."

I didn't get to finish, as another of Luke's kisses stopped my words.

"Let's get one thing clear, Kaker Mayne," Luke interrupted me, "I'm not the kind of man to go running back to mother every time my wife gets a little crazy."

I had to laugh at that.

"And you sure have been a little crazy this summer," he said, laughing with me, and pulling me with him onto my too-small bed.

Since the *crazy* didn't seem to be going away anytime soon, I was happy to have confirmation that Luke Mayne was not easily scared off.

"Ah-hem," Daniel cleared his throat to get my attention. He had a quizzical smile on his face, which mirrored my own goofy grin. I hoped he wasn't able to read my thoughts.

Shaking my head, I cleared the memories of Luke's sweet homecoming—or at least enough of them to remember what I had been talking about with Daniel.

"All right," I conceded to Daniel, waving my hand to the greater audience. "You all decide what color you want, and make it happen. Talking about paint makes me cranky."

I avoided looking at Daniel, because I knew he and the twins would be rolling their eyes, and I just didn't have the energy for it.

"Make Nan happy," I said finally, "that's all I ask."

Walking back to the lodge from the A-Frame, my phone rang. It was Lilian Atwater.

Of course, I thought, let's top this day off with another humdinger of a conversation.

"Kay," she said in her clipped, authoritative tone.

"What can I do for you, Lilian?" I asked her, trying to skip the chit chat. Today had been a rollercoaster of emotions, and Lilian was the big dip at the bottom—the one that made your stomach flip.

"The Atwater's were counting on Bella to attend our final soiree of the summer tomorrow afternoon… but Max has told me you won't allow it!" she declared.

Her little *Maxie* didn't get his way, and mummy was going to make it all better. No matter who she had to bully and push around.

"That's right," I said.

After a pause, Lilian continued. "Kay, I don't know what I've done to earn your disdain… but we shouldn't let your little notions interfere with the children and their fun."

She was right, I realized.

She didn't know why I was keeping Bella away from her home, because I'd never told her. Aside from the incident on Daniel's deck, I had not stood up to Lilian, or even Max for that matter. Not about the drinking on the jet ski, or about Max pressuring Wren.

I had been afraid of conflict at the beginning of August, and now that the girls would be leaving soon, I was hoping it would all just go away on its own. And maybe it would, if I left it alone. But should I?

Weren't my nieces worth a *water dance*—and my protection? Weren't Lilian and Max intruders on Tad and Selby's little birds, who were entrusted to me?

Having them call me Kaker was no longer the goal. If I wanted to earn my aunt stripes, I needed to stand tall and do what was best for these girls while they were under my roof. Just as Fitz and Raya counted on the watchful eye of Gram, and June, and Zeke while I was growing up.

"Lilian, your son's idea of fun is reckless, and not appropriate for my nieces," I said at last, so Lilian would know where I stood. "Max likes to drink alcohol, and he doesn't like to drink alone."

Lilian was silent.

"And I haven't found you to be a reliable chaperone," I said. "My brother and his wife would expect more from the homes their daughters spend time at."

Including my own, I thought.

"I don't know what you're talking about," Lilian sputtered.

"You already know that Max and Bella were drinking wine here outside one of my cabins—stolen wine," I said. "While at your house, Max brought a flask out on the jet skis, and pressured the other kids to join him."

"Who did you hear that from?" Lilian asked, "I demand to know!"

I ignored her demands.

"Like Max, Bella is only 17. She is too young for drinking of any kind," I said instead. "Both in the eyes of the law, and her family."

There was a pause, and I could hear Lilian breathing heavily.

"Lies," Lilian said before hanging up.

Let the chips fall where they may.

38

We lake it here.
We lake it a lot.
-KERBY LODGE GUEST BOOK-

The next afternoon was warm. I tried to un-tense my muscles by floating in the lake. My peaceful countenance was failing me, however, as I wobbled from side to side in the water.

"No wonder," I said to myself, "look at this belly!" Sitting on the sand bar, I reached down and cupped the sides of my normally flat tummy, which had popped a bit from all the cookies I'd been eating.

Stress eating!

I had been anxious this summer, no doubt, and I was paying a high price—gaining weight, snapping at family and friends, and in general, compromising my health.

"I need stress management," I said out loud to the lake, "not comfort food."

But at the same time, Mitch's mac and cheese appeared in my head like an old friend.

Focusing all my attention on my sore stomach muscles, I tried to relax. It seems I had been holding these muscles taut for all of August, waiting for a shoe to drop. The other shoe, or the first shoe... I wasn't sure which. All I knew was that my life seemed full of big heavy shoes, which had all been dancing a jig in my stomach for weeks.

142

Leaning back on my elbows, I took a deep breath while gazing up at the gently swaying pine trees. The same ones I had wanted to cut down. And suddenly, it all seemed so clear.

"Hollis was right," I whispered in the direction of the pines. Creating a wedding venue would be opening a big fat never ending can of worms. I'd much rather have the trees.

And at that, I exhaled a month's worth of tension, and glided into an effortless float.

Is that it?

Is that what's been troubling me this summer?

I silently asked myself this, not daring to speak out loud and disturb this delicate balance and peaceful feeling.

Pieces in a puzzle, was the answer that came back to me, as the gentle swells of the water pushed and pulled the stress out of my sore aching muscles. Creating a wedding venue was just one unresolved issue of many this summer, and it was now resolved. The rest would be behind me in days.

The Grays would leave in the morning.

Gram's house was almost finished.

Alice Fanning had agreed to watch the inn this fall.

Luke was home, and was at the school, preparing for students.

Order was being restored to life and lodge.

The Atwater's would soon be gone, following their end of summer party. It was going on right now, I imagined. I told Bella that I didn't want her to go, and she seemed to take my denial in stride, which shows how much closer she and I have gotten this summer.

Bella very maturely told me that she had fun with the girls in town the day before, more fun than with Max. She asked if she could go with Patti Lee to the movies, and I agreed, letting her once again take the Jeep.

Just as I did yesterday, I would give Sue a call to verify, as soon as I found a spare minute—it was no longer urgent. Bella had been demonstrating to me that I could trust her. And when it came down to it, it was really Max I didn't trust, not Bella.

Wren was not interested in the movies and stayed behind. She wanted to spend her last days reading, swimming, and playing with Cody.

Tad and Selby would arrive in two days. I'd have to put them in Mum and Dad's bedroom of the apartment, after pushing a few boxes around.

I hoped June and Zeke would make it, but wasn't sure where they'd stay. Maybe we'd have a cancellation in one of the guestrooms. If not, Luke and I would sleep on the apartment sofas for a few nights and give them our room.

The Mayne's would also be here soon, and would be staying with Daniel. *Ugh. Staying with Daniel.*

Talking to Daniel about moving out of the A-Frame altogether was the final piece of my impossible summer puzzle. It was one of those puzzles without a clear picture—just one solid color, where you don't know where to begin.

But I would put that to rights over Labor Day.

I'd simply say, "Daniel, you'll always have a home at Kerby Lodge, the lodge you helped me save, but it can no longer be the A-Frame. It's nothing personal. It's just business."

Walking up the path from the beach in the afternoon sun, I considered veering over to the carriage house to talk to Jennifer. I wanted to be sure she and Patrick would be coming to my Labor Day weekend cookout.

Also, I wanted to nail down a day when we could all go to lunch or dinner and hang out—have a few long overdue laughs.

At first, it was Daniel who made up our foursome with Jenny and Patrick, and we had a great time together. When I married Luke, I was worried that either Daniel or Luke would feel left out, but quickly realized that men don't play those games.

The five of us got together when we could, and as Daniel's business picked up, Luke seamlessly took his place at our dinner parties and game nights. Now, I'd have to organize a few gatherings with the six of us—and bring Beth into the mix.

Suddenly exhausted, I veered instead towards the lodge to enjoy an afternoon nap. These naps would be sorely missed once I started substitute teaching in just a few days' time.

It wasn't long before I fell into a deep sleep, aided by the sound of gentle waves splashing on the shore of the Kerby Lodge beach. In my dreams, the waves were joined by the *buzz buzzing* of a little bee—which grew louder, until it became a swarm.

Buzz buzz.

In my dream, I heard the low voices of men—were they talking to the bees?

Buzz buzz.

When I heard a deep voice shout "timber," I realized I wasn't dreaming about bees at all, but my grove of pine trees coming down. Thankfully, that would never happen with Chip's busy schedule. I'd call him soon.

"Call off the hounds," I'd tell Chip, and we'd have a good laugh at how annoying I'd been all summer, and how Chip would certainly never get rich off of Kerby Lodge.

144

I'd explain that every bride deserves one perfect day—her wedding day—before all the chaos of life unfolds. And after this summer, I am completely convinced Kerby Lodge is not the place for that perfect day. Kerby Lodge is a place to celebrate all of life's perfectly imperfect days. The "for worse" days, and the "for poorer" days.

The "in sickness" days, as with the Gray family.

My wedding reception was perfect, because this is my backyard. This is where I feel closest to my Mum and Dad. But to every other bride in the world, I say: *Get outta here! Go somewhere else!* Get married where every detail is thought of, and then go live a little.

After your first fight, after you take your goofy wedding gifts for a drive, and have hot dogs for dinner three nights in a row—then come to Kerby Lodge. Try not to twist your ankle on an acorn, or trip over a tree root.

I smiled as I began stirring from my nap and heard it again, "timber!"

When my body vibrated with a deep thud, my eyes shot open. This was no dream, I realized, and that was no bee.

Looking out the window, I was shocked to see Chip and his crew in my grove, where, to my horror, they had successfully taken down three pines. They were poised to begin cutting down a fourth.

"No... no... no..." I yelled at the top of my sleep-filled lungs as I sprinted to the door.

Hair flying, I held my shoes in my hand as I ran barefoot. Projecting myself outside like a ball bearing fired from a slingshot, I proceeded to step down hard on a sharp splinter of wood. I shouted in pain so loudly through the noise that everyone looked my way.

Chip held his hand up, and his crew put their chain saws down.

"Kay?" he asked, "what is it—is something wrong?"

"Stop... stop now," I said, as I backed up to one of the trees protectively.

"Kay, you've been calling me all summer to do this," Chip said, gesturing to the trees. "We had a cancellation... so, here we are."

"I see that," I said, trying to catch my breath.

Chip was frustrated, I could tell. My arms were getting sore from trying to hold onto the scratchy pine and save its life.

"You don't have to chain yourself to that tree, Kay," Chip said. "This is your property. All you have to do is tell me you've changed your mind."

"I changed... my mind..." I said, panting and trying to catch my breath.

Chip and the crew stood still, watching to see if I was joking.

"All right fellas, let's pack up and move out," Chip shouted at last.

He walked over to me and breathed a deep sign of resignation. Then he took my arm and navigated me away from the tree, and away from the gnarly slivers of raw wood.

He continued to hold my arm as I limped over to one of the fallen pines where we both sat down. Chip lifted my foot and carefully brushed off the wood chip that adhered there. Taking the shoes out of my hands, he gently slipped them on my feet.

"I'm so sorry Chip," I said. "Since I hadn't heard from you, I thought I had plenty of time to call and cancel. I just can't do this—I don't know what I was thinking."

I dropped my head in my hands.

Chip placed his hand on my back and gave me a few clumsy pats. "No worries, Kay," he said, "not much damage done here. We'll move on to the next job."

We both looked at the grove, which was intact for the most part.

"I'll come back this fall and chip these three trees," he said, with a grudging smile on his face. "But don't text me or bug me. I might need a little break from the Kerby's."

I smiled back at him weakly and said, "okay, except that Bella is with Patti Lee today, so you'll likely see another Kerby before the day is out."

Chip's smile faded immediately.

"That's not possible, Kay," he said. "Patti Lee is away, staying with her grandmother. I drove her there myself, last night."

39

A little drama here this summer, just saying.
Fitz and Raya never had drama.
-KERBY LODGE GUEST BOOK-

Where was Bella?

My thoughts were reeling as I began walking back to the lodge—picking up speed with each step. I pulled out my phone and called her, but she didn't answer. I wanted to call Luke, but before alarming him, I'd ask Wren if she had any ideas where Bella might have gone.

At this time of day, Wren was probably helping Jennifer close the carriage house.

If Wren didn't know where Bella was, I decided, then I'd call Luke. And then, I would call the police. My stomach lurched just thinking about making that call.

Chip drove past me on the Kerby Lodge road. He waved, but I was too preoccupied to wave back. In the background, I barely registered the familiar sounds of laughter and yelling coming from Lake Michigan. The voices were drowned out by the motor of a boat, or a jet ski.

It made me think about the Atwater's cocktail party, and how Wren and Bella had been riding too fast with Max—an inebriated Max, I found out later. Whoever thought it was impossible to get injured on the water with jet skis was misinformed.

147

As I passed the lodge, I glanced down at the beach. Indeed, there was a jet ski that seemed to be heading towards Kerby Lodge and the sand bar, but its closeness must have been an optical illusion caused by the bright sun. Any time now, they would surely turn and ride parallel to the shore. I didn't have time to stop and watch—I needed to find my missing niece.

There weren't many swimmers in the water that I could see. It was dinner time around the lodge, and guests were either eating in their cabins, or out at restaurants with their families. Everyone loved to stroll through the town at the end of summer, eating ice cream from the Dairy Dip, and shopping the sidewalk sales.

The sounds got louder, and closer.

"Someone is going way too fast," I said to Jennifer as I reached the carriage house, and saw my friend looking with concern towards the lake.

At that moment, Stuart and Joy Gray came running towards us both.

"Have you seen him—have you seen Cody?" They tripped over each other's words.

My mind drew a blank as I tried to process that both Bella and Cody were missing.

"We were packing the car, and… and…" Stuart spoke with great urgency.

These two, so lethargic and removed these past few weeks were now moving quickly on legs that had been dragging around like cement pylons. These voices that had been deadpan were now animated, as they frantically searched for their missing son.

The son who had gone unnoticed by them for two weeks.

The jet ski was getting much closer now, which seemed improbable. It was against the law to exceed safe speeds within a certain distance from the shore in Michigan. And it was dangerous. If the driver of the jet ski didn't turn soon and head back into deeper waters…

"Is he with Alice?" I asked Joy and Stuart, though she never watched Cody in the afternoon. "Is he with Wren?"

Wren came in off the beach a while ago, they said. The little boy was not with her.

I began to wonder if the two disappearances had any connection, when piercing screams came up from the lake. With whiplash precision, the screams captured everyone's attention as we turned towards the Kerby Lodge beach to see what was going on.

The jet ski's motor had revved, then stopped abruptly before the shrieking began.

Alice and Wren raced outside from the lodge just then, looking wildly towards the water. These were not playful screams. That much was certain.

148

The blood in my veins turned to ice, and I froze.

Jennifer reacted immediately—switching from store owner to trained first responder in the blink of an eye. While the Gray's held on to each other in terror, Jennifer was already tearing down the lawn, towards the water.

I followed after her.

"Call 911, Kay!" she shouted over her shoulder. "Tell them a jet ski hit a child."

Stunned, I somehow did as Jennifer told me to.

As for Stuart and Joy, once the realization that the child Jennifer mentioned might be their own missing son, they added their screams to those coming from the lake, as they ran down the bluff to the water.

I said a quick prayer for Cody, and for whoever had hit him—a jet ski was powerful, like a charging rhinoceros. And little Cody was so small and fragile. Surely someone will pay a hefty price for the rest of their life if Cody is badly injured.

Or worse.

After sending a quick text to Luke, saying *COME HOME I NEED YOU*, there was nothing to do but head towards the lake; towards the cacophony of anguish, and whatever awaited me there. Hearing the sirens heading our way, I felt thankful the EMTs had been close by.

In a scene I will remember for the rest of my life, I could see that the thrill-seeking pair in the water—still screaming next to an overturned jet ski on the sand bar; next to a limp and lifeless Cody Gray—was none other than Max… and Bella.

My legs buckled and I nearly fell onto the grassy sand.

Turning away from the scene, I grasped my stomach and violently threw up.

Bella hadn't gone to the movies. She went to see Max.

I felt more than saw *whooshing* movements on either side of me, which turned out to be Patrick and his partner Joe, running towards the water and Jennifer. They carried a stretcher, and first aid kits.

As he ran to the shore, Patrick talked into the two-way radio clipped to his lapel.

Jennifer stood waist deep in Lake Michigan, holding Cody Gray in a floating position with one hand, and motioned for Stuart and Joy to remain on the beach with the other hand.

Alice was there, with her arms around a sobbing Joy Gray—comforting and steadying her. Cody's little body did not move.

Patrick and Joe splashed into the lake towards Cody, and helped Jennifer secure him to a stretcher. They placed an oxygen mask on his lifeless little face, and Jennifer began squeezing air into his lungs as she helped Joe carry the stretcher towards the ambulance.

Patrick made his way to the still screaming Max and Bella.

Max was sitting on top of the sandbar in an awkward sideways position, doubled over in pain or shock. Bella stood apart from him, as if consciously distancing herself from Max.

Seconds later, two police officers strode into the lake. I hadn't noticed their sirens amongst the screams and cries that filled the shoreline. Taking my eyes off of Bella for a split second, I turned to look over my shoulder. The police car flashers were blinking wildly from the parking pad, as were the lights on the ambulance.

Guests came out of cabins and guestrooms, and quietly lined up between the trees. Some sat on the bluff, watching the disaster unfold.

I didn't know what comfort I could be to the Gray's, and so I stayed near them but didn't attempt to engage them. What could I possibly say? At any rate, they soon turned and ran after the EMTs and the stretcher with their son on it.

A second ambulance arrived as the first one left for the hospital, and two more EMTs made their way to the lake. A boat pulled up to the sandbar, near where the police officers stood in the water. It was the Coast Guard.

The first ambulance departed, taking the screaming sirens and the screaming Grays with it—leaving Bella and Max. Only Max was screaming now. He seemed very small. As the police and the EMTs spoke with him, I could see that he couldn't stand up on his own, and so they helped him onto a stretcher with flotation devices on the sides. Max writhed in pain, and couldn't straighten his left leg.

As two EMTs and one police officer worked to strap Max down, he fought and rolled from side to side—in pain or in protestation.

Max's arms flailed wildly, and he had to be restrained.

The officers were not allowing me to enter the water, and so I stayed on shore and kept a bead on Bella. She had become completely still, and only nodded her head slightly as the police and coast guard officers spoke with her.

I was aware of Wren nearby on the shore, sobbing as Alice held onto her.

"What can I do to help?" I looked to my side, and saw Chip standing there. Of course, he had barely left Kerby Lodge when he passed the oncoming sirens, and turned around.

Without hesitating, I said "go pick up Lilian and Skip, and bring them to the hospital. They're in no condition to drive."

Chip nodded and ran back up the bluff towards his truck.

As a screaming Max was being carried towards the ambulance, I pulled out my phone and searched for a call I received the day before, then pressed the callback button. After a few rings, a very inebriated Lilian Atwater answered.

"Yesh…" she said.

I could hear laughter in the background, and glasses tinkling.

"Lilian, listen carefully," I said. "Max is badly hurt, but he'll be okay."

"Wha…" her reactions were slow.

"Do not drive," I said in as authoritative a tone as I could muster, a tone I should have used more with Bella, "Chip is on his way to bring you and Skip to the hospital."

After I was confident that she understood, I hung up.

Then I turned my attention to my niece.

40

We hope all is okay.
-KERBY LODGE GUEST BOOK-

There are things the mind won't let you handle all at once—I discovered this 13 years ago, when my parents passed away, just days apart.

I was able to blessedly compartmentalize the magnitude of what I had lost, so that I could take care of the tasks at hand. The funerals, the settling of the estate, and the comforting of others. It wasn't until everyone had gone home that the grief was doled out to me in increasingly larger servings, over several years.

And except for summers, when I had Aunt June and Uncle Zeke with me, I isolated myself and dealt with these emotions alone, until they overwhelmed me—and I slipped into a depressed, lethargic state.

It all came back to me when I met the Gray family.

Stuart, Joy, and Cody Gray had just begun to deal with the magnitude of their loss. They had come to Kerby Lodge to rest and to heal, finding an unlikely support system in the good and pure hearts of sweet Wren, and Alice Fanning.

How horrible it would be if the healing waters of Lake Michigan and the shores of Kerby Lodge came to be their undoing.

"Can you believe it," people would be saying for years, "the accident at Kerby Lodge?"

They came to heal, and then...

They were packing to leave, and then…

You can't make this stuff up, people would say.

Sadly, they'd be right.

The Gray's depended on our staff to an extreme level. They barely spoke to us in the two weeks they were here, let alone to the other families. They didn't make friends. They didn't trust strangers to watch Cody while they packed their car. Instead, they put their trust in the blue skies and calm day.

They put their trust in little Cody himself, and the personal flotation device he was wearing. Thinking that the only danger was the water.

They didn't see Bella as a danger.

Or Max.

Luke and Daniel saw Max as a danger, from day one. But I saw him as more of a nuisance. Either way, Max's nature was overshadowed by my own desire to make up for lost time, and become the girls' favorite, fun-loving aunt.

Tad and Selby trusted me to take care of their daughters for a few short weeks while they travelled, and yet here was Bella, lying on a bed in the hospital, suffering from shock. The doctor gave her a mild sedative which would allow her body and mind to rest for a short blessed while.

Wren sat in the waiting room. Alice Fanning's arms held tight around her as she shook with fear and anguish.

I imagined my brother and his wife walking into the hospital right now. What condition would they find these girls in after their unforgettable summer at Kerby Lodge? Oh, the damage I had allowed.

The girls would never come back. Tad would never come back.

As I sat next to a sleeping Bella, running my hand over her arm, Luke sat next to me.

I felt bad for Skip and Lilian. Surely they knew Max was drinking while driving the watercraft, but probably thought, *what can happen on the open water?* At worst, he'd tumble off the jet ski into the lake and have to climb back on, but that's not so bad, is it?

They likely didn't know that Max had so much destructive anger inside of him.

They didn't know Max needed to win an end-of-summer battle against *'lil 'ol me*, Kay Kerby Mayne. That he needed to show me where Bella really was, by driving the loud jet ski close to Kerby Lodge.

See, Kaker? She's with me—this is what I think he wanted to say.

I imagined Max pulling out his silver flask to drink his courage. It must have felt like his last chance to feel like a man in front of the Kerby women, and his own troubled parents.

Max knew the sandbar was close by. I remember the day I saw his jet ski parked there while he swam with the girls. But his reactions were slow. His depth perception was skewed by the alcohol in his system, coupled with the glare of the late afternoon sun, which notoriously reflects off the ripples.

I imagined heavy drops of Lake Michigan splashing and sheeting off of Max's sunglasses as he pounded the water. Maybe he thought he saw a ball, or a beach toy bobbing in the shallows, but didn't think much of it—it would get out of his way, not the other way around.

He was Max freaking Atwater!

Yes, the Atwater family was to be pitied. There was no winner here today.

Our community hospital is small, and the triage area is divided only by curtains. Everyone, I'm sure, could clearly hear the Kerby Lodge tragedy unfolding in increments. First, Doctor Petersen came in to see if Bella was awake. He told me, in quiet tones, that physically she was completely fine. "She'll wake up soon," he said, and then left.

To what? I wondered, but sighed from relief.

Max came back from X-ray. His screams had turned to loud incomprehensible moans that reverberated off the cinderblock walls. I was glad Bella was asleep.

Everyone within earshot heard that Max broke his left leg in two places, and would have a long, painful recovery after surgery. The doctor told his wailing mother that Max had a lot of alcohol in his system, but once that wore off, they could begin to give him pain medication.

"Your kid is *schnockered*," I heard the doctor say, with his blunt bedside manner.

Just outside of our own curtain, a police officer talked to Skip and Lilian. He told them that Max was facing serious charges of a minor in possession of alcohol, in tandem with operating a watercraft while under the influence, and exceeding speed limits close to shore.

The officer said there could be other charges as well, once the condition of the young child was disclosed. He recommended they call an attorney.

As Lilian whined and burbled, Skip Atwater excused himself to do just that.

The last sound I remember hearing before my own loud wails filled the area, and before I fainted and nearly slid to the hospital floor—and would have but for Luke—was a little boy's sing-song voice.

"I was *froze*, Mommy," Cody Gray was saying, "I couldn't move."

The overlapping voices of Stuart and Joy Gray as they responded to Cody were overjoyed and animated. "You couldn't *move* Cody? Were you *scared?* What *happened?*"

"I was scared, but Bella turned the boat," Cody said.

41

The ambulances freaked us out a bit.
Someone's vacation was ruined.
-KERBY LODGE GUEST BOOK-

Bella turned the boat.

The statement she gave to the police and the Coast Guard while standing in the water was the same as she gave upon waking in the hospital.

She had lied about going to the movies, and went to the Atwater's for one last jet ski ride with Max. Bella glanced at me sheepishly as she admitted this. Once they were on the watercraft, she said, she suspected Max had been drinking and realized she'd made a big mistake. She asked to go back.

No, she didn't take a sip of alcohol at any time.

No, Max wouldn't go back, he told her, not until they went past Kerby Lodge.

Max seemed wild, Bella said. She saw little Cody on the sandbar and tugged on Max's arm to get him to turn. He couldn't seem to hear her over the loud engine as the jet ski pounded time and again into the water.

Cody was frozen in place, watching in terror as the jet ski flew towards him.

The sandbar was near, Bella knew, and prayed it would protect the little boy—even if it meant great harm to her and Max if they slammed into it. She panicked as they got very close to Cody, and reached out to pull hard on the right handle, causing the jet ski to flip over.

Bella flew off the back, safely into the water. At the same time, the jet ski tilted hard to the left, pinning Max between it and the sand bar just long enough to crush his leg.

In the commotion, it seems, little Cody fainted and slid into the lake, but the jet ski never made contact. Though it came very, very close. Thankfully, Cody's life jacket buoyed the little guy until Jennifer reached him and kept his head from submerging.

No one spoke as Luke drove us all home from the hospital. The girls were subdued, huddled together in the back seat of the SUV.

I pulled out my phone and sent a quick text message to Tad—though I knew they were likely in the air, on the first of a few flights that would bring them to Kerby Lodge the day after the next.

"Girls are great," I said, "they miss you."

Then, remembering how mad I was at Jennifer for withholding information about the lodge while I was away, I added, "There was a jet ski accident on the lake today involving Bella, but she was not harmed. Only shaken. Details upon arrival."

We pulled into Kerby Lodge around midnight, and I could see welcoming lights coming from the apartment and great room. I certainly hoped no one from my family had arrived early for the Labor Day weekend. I was just not ready to be a host.

The outside air was cold, I realized, stepping out of the car. Warm days and cool nights were not uncommon towards the end of August.

And as we walked into the lodge, I saw a sight for sore eyes—Daniel was there, along with Beth and Stace. And both Hollis and Alice Fanning.

Everybody quietly embraced the girls, and new tears were shed by everyone. Hollis and Stace encouraged my nieces to each take a hot shower, then come have a bite to eat as they decompressed among friends and family.

"I know where your aunt keeps her secret stash of your grandfather's flannel shirts," Stace said, causing Bella and Wren to smile a little for the first time all day.

Daniel and Beth, and Alice, all had warm hugs for me, too. Beth had brought a platter of sandwiches and a pot of beef barley soup.

"Sit by the fire, Kaker," Daniel said as he guided me to the wing chairs. "You've had quite a shock. I made some fresh coffee."

I tried to smile at my brother-in-law, who had become such a giving and sensitive man after recovering from the trauma of losing his beloved job two years ago. But fresh tears streamed down my face instead. Daniel looked helplessly over at Luke, who came over to wrap his arms around me.

After a few minutes, I sat by the fire and tried to stop shaking. Luke placed one of the warm wool blankets on my lap, as Beth brought me a mug of soup.

"Thank you, Beth," I said through teary eyes, and she smiled and nodded.

"Kaker, did you really faint at the hospital?" Wren was asking as she walked into the room. She wore leggings, and one of my favorite flannel shirts that Fitz used to wear. She was so tall and lovely, that even in an oversized shirt and damp red hair, she took my breath away.

"She did, Wren," Luke answered for me, as he reached over and took my hand. "But the doctor checked her out, and she's fine. Everybody's fine!" he said as he exhaled with relief.

All I could do was nod. Everybody's fine, no thanks to me. I had saved the pines, but not my own family.

When Bella entered the room, she was a little more subdued than Wren, though no less lovely in a flannel shirt and leggings. Hollis and Stace were waiting on the girls, bringing them hot coffees with sugar, along with soup and sandwiches. And blankets.

I was so glad to see them eating and taking warm sips of the sugary coffee. They had both been shaking from the trauma of the day.

After a short time, Alice and Hollis came over and quietly said their goodbyes to me—they were going to bring a few sandwiches to the hospital for Stuart and Joy before going home to their own beds. The doctors wanted to keep Cody overnight, and of course his parents refused to leave his side.

"They'll come by in the morning for their things," Alice said, and then followed Hollis.

"We're going to head home too," Stace said quietly to me. She came to sit on the hearth so we could talk.

Everyone was speaking in such quiet tones, it reminded me of the visitations for my parents at the funeral home. But even though tragedy had been averted today, there was a pensive and fragile air in the room befitting such a close call.

"Thank you, and thank Beth again for the wonderful comfort food, Stace," I said. "It's just what we needed tonight."

"You're welcome, Kay," she said. "Anyway, it seems like we're all becoming one big family," she added, looking over at Daniel and Beth who were sitting and holding hands.

"Be careful," I smiled weakly at her, "families are messy."

She smiled back, "you're preaching to the choir."

I allowed myself a genuine laugh at that, which the room desperately needed.

"Oh, and by the way, Gram's house, *your* house, is almost done," Stace said. "You and Luke can move in soon—two or three days. Is there anything else you want us to do there, besides the things we've talked about?

"Yes, there is," I said, "I'm glad you're sitting down."

42

Thank you sincerely for everything,
From the sandy bottom of our beach bag.
-KERBY LODGE GUEST BOOK-

Seeing little Cody bound happily out of his car in front of the lodge the next morning was good medicine for Bella and Wren, and for Alice especially. She had been distraught at the idea of Cody being injured *on her watch*, as she said.

As for the little guy, he seemed to wonder what all the fuss was about. After all, he'd been at Kerby Lodge for two whole weeks, and nobody paid him much notice. Now, his parents wouldn't let him out of their sight. And all the other ladies—or *wadies*, as he said with his childhood lisp—were falling all over him.

Alice presented Cody with a plastic lunch box. It was filled with a few cars and toys that her son used to play with, and a coloring book. "There are stickers in there too," she said, "so you can decorate the box."

I gave him a Kerby Lodge hoodie to wear home, in case he got cold.

Bella and Wren gave him a brown bag with a juice box for the road, and snacks.

Then Cody, head spinning from his newfound power, completely terrified his captive audience by asking if he could go for "one more *thwim*" before they left.

I could see everyone's jaw drop open as they got ready to scream a collective *NO,* but to Stuart's credit, he smiled and nodded his head at Cody, and at me, and at Bella and Wren, and at Joy and Alice, and said, "let's all go for a swim."

And that's how Stuart Gray, grieving father of one, grateful father of another, taught us all an important lesson about getting back on a bike after falling off.

Rain clouds rolled in after the Gray's left Kerby Lodge. The girls went to change out of their wet bathing suits, and sleep for a little bit. It was that kind of day, following one we wished to forget.

Instead of heading to the school, Luke stayed with me.

He and I took our light lunch of Beth's soup and sandwiches, and went to sit on the sun porch to watch the waves gather on the lake. Walking through the darkening great room, I stopped to turn on a few lamps. I could smell the pine floors, the stones on the fireplace, and the rain moving in from the west.

"I should have listened to you, Luke," I said, sitting closely next to my husband on one of the recovered rattan loveseats, "then none of this would have happened."

Like the storm system, the regrets were settling in—and about to break loose.

"We don't know that," he said.

"I didn't watch Bella closely enough," I said, in a voice that was just this side of a sob.

"You're her aunt, Kaker," he said, "not her jailer."

Luke was gazing out the window, a million miles away, it seemed.

"Wait… what do you mean? You're the one who said I should be stricter," I said.

"Just shows you," Luke said, smiling faintly, "I don't have all the answers."

"Well, that's frightening," I said, "because if you don't… and I don't… who does?"

Luke just turned to look at the water and shrugged.

"I'm a fraud, Kaker," Luke practically whispered.

After a few minutes, Luke very quietly told me how the events of the week had badly shaken him. He realized now that dispensing advice was the easy part, but that real-life events were another matter, and could actually—not just theoretically—be devastating.

"I'm all talk when it comes to other people's kids," he said, "I've got plenty of advice for my students and their parents, Kaker. But what if it was our daughter, lying to us, and out drinking with boys? Or what if it was our son in the water, with a jet ski coming at him?"

I squeezed Luke's hand.

"I think now," he went on, "that maybe I changed schools every two years to avoid this very thing. To avoid getting involved, or getting hurt."

Helplessly, Luke turned to look at me. There were tears in his eyes.

"Look at this picture of your grandfather, Fitzwilliam Kerby." I held a photo up for the girls to see. "He was a civil engineer, you know, and very smart. And very handsome," I said, setting the photo in a pile.

"I see you in him, Bella," I went on. "He was tall and willowy, with the same chestnut hair you have. He was known around here for choosing his words carefully. When he spoke, people listened."

After the girls woke from their naps and ate lunch, I pulled the box of old photos out again and sat squarely in the middle of the burnt orange sofa in the great room. They had rejected looking through these photos before, calling it a lame *camp craft*, but they were much more open today.

Without any cajoling, they grabbed their blankets and sat down on either side of me—looking with interest at the pictures, and listening to the stories I had to tell. Luke came in with a tray of hot cocoas, and after we thanked him, I nodded my head towards the door and smiled.

Luke winked at me and grabbed his keys to head to the school.

"You have the same self-assured way of capturing an audience, Bella," I continued. "As you get older, you'll learn to choose your words and actions carefully, just as Fitz did."

Bella looked up at me with the faintest of fragile smiles, and before she knew what was coming, I leaned over and gently kissed her on the forehead.

She allowed it.

"I see every one of these people in both you girls," I said, "Fitz and Raya, your father, Gram... and a little bit of myself."

"We are all your strong foundation," I told them, "holding you up."

They would make mistakes, for sure. But they could not possibly fall.

43

Give a man a fish and he will eat for a day. Teach him to fish,
and he will sit in his boat all day, eating sandwiches.
-KERBY LODGE GUEST BOOK-

And so it was that on the very last day of their visit, before their parents returned, I had Bella and Wren exactly where I'd wanted them from the beginning.

But what a high price to get them to this point.

They were staying close to me, and the three of us found ourselves laughing and talking about everything. We looked at more family photos, especially after the girls found pictures of their dad during his childhood at Kerby Lodge.

"Look at this one, Wren," Bella said, holding up a prized picture, "Daddy is standing inside the carriage house—right where Jennifer's cash register sits!"

I encouraged them to make a pile of photos to show Tad the next day, when he got here. "I think he's forgotten how much fun he used to have at Kerby Lodge," I said. Bella and Wren nodded, then enthusiastically began documenting Tad's young life.

There were pictures of Tad with Raya and Fitz, and many with me.

There were a few good ones of Tad riding with Gram in her golf cart.

"Look at this one, Kaker," Bella said, handing me a photo of a young Tad, standing in a group of boys down by the tire swing that hangs over the lake.

Something about the group caught my eye. Two of the young boys looked very familiar—until I realized it was Luke and Daniel, from their long-ago vacation. The one that brought Daniel back to the lodge, his *happy place*, two years ago.

"My goodness," I managed, with a large lump in my throat.

I stood up and placed the photo on the mantle of the fireplace, where it wouldn't get lost in one of the many piles the girls were making.

It was so good to see Bella relaxed and happy, recovering from the shock of the day before. Of course, spending a little bit of time in the lake this morning with a happy and healthy Cody Gray was good medicine.

Wren, too, could easily have fallen into a guilt-ridden depression if Cody was harmed. I know this little bird who wore her heart on her sleeve felt in some way responsible for the child, in spite of my attempts at shielding her from taking on too much.

This happiness we three felt was only temporary, I knew from experience. Emotions were bound to surface—in increasingly larger waves as the girls were able to handle them.

They came sooner than I expected.

Bella became very quiet all of a sudden, and then spoke without looking up. She held a picture in her hands of Tad and I out on the sand bar. "I was so frightened on the jet ski with Max," she said quietly. "He was driving so fast, and he seemed like a different person from the one I thought I knew."

I held my breath and willed her to continue—to get it all out in the open.

"I didn't want him to think I wasn't cool while we were drinking on Daniel's deck, and at his house, but now… I wish with all my heart I had been stronger, like you Kaker."

I nodded, but I was floored.

She thinks I'm strong.

"I'm just glad I got a second chance, and didn't hurt that little boy," Bella sobbed. "He has his whole life ahead of him!"

"As do you, dear one," I said.

"But I hurt Max," she said, voice shaking.

It's true that Max Atwater would have a long recovery from his leg injuries—his senior year of high school would be much different than the one he had planned. But maybe, just maybe, he would have a recovery of another kind. Perhaps he could break free from his addiction to alcohol, and to his own internal anger.

Maybe Max and his parents could experience a wake-up call from this accident, and draw closer to the things that really matter in life.

"No, you saved Max," I said. "When you saved Cody, you also saved Max."

164

Someday Bella would fully grasp just how momentous turning the boat really was. If she hadn't grabbed the handle of the jet ski when she did, there would be no farewell swim with Cody. No smiling parents.

The little rag-tag group of women who made their way down the soft pine needle path to Lake Michigan—who tentatively stepped into the water, only to be bombarded by the splashes of a four-year-old—that healing time never would have happened.

If Bella hadn't turned the boat, Stuart and Joy Gray, who were just beginning to surface from one devastating loss, would be comatose with grief. Max would have sobered up just long enough to understand the consequences of his actions, then spent the rest of his life trying to forget again.

"His leg will heal, and he'll have his whole life," I said, "to decide how he wants to live."

Bella cried into my arms.

When she could speak, Bella asked, "will you tell my parents what happened?"

"You will," I answered. "You'll find the words, and the right time, and tell them everything. They love you beyond measure, and you can trust them."

Bella nodded.

As I treasured this closeness, I thought of Tad and Selby arriving at Kerby Lodge tomorrow, to find that their girls had summer adventures none of us could have anticipated.

Maybe my brother and his wife won't be shocked. I'm sure, as parents of two teenagers, they've had their moments; maybe that's why they needed a vacation by themselves.

Maybe I'm the only one surprised and unprepared for the drama, and the emotion, and the lies, and the deception, and the insecurities of teenagers. The way they can turn on their charm when it suits them, and become needy children when they're frightened by the world.

They were like summer storms, devastating and glorious at the same time. Here one minute and gone the next. Capable of both destruction and breathtaking beauty.

The girls were right when they said my perception of them was shallow—they had been sweet faces on a Christmas card photo every year, and not much more. But that would never be the case again. This visit was nothing like I'd planned, and nearly came to a tragic ending. Instead, it would end on a high note. I'd make sure of that.

At that thought, I turned the subject around.

"Let's talk about our menu for the first annual Labor Day weekend cookout," I said dramatically, drawing the girls in as my co-conspirators. "After all, when I'm old and gray, you two will be in charge of this shindig, so let's do it up right from the start."

Bella sat up with a grin on her face and said, "too late, Kaker, you already have a few silvery hairs. Do you want to hand us the reigns now?"

I feigned indignance and playfully swatted Bella's hand as it was pointing to my strawberry blonde waves—if I did have a few gray hairs, it was no doubt because of these two.

"I'll make the sweet tea, and biscuits," Bella said, "Wren can make cheese straws."

"Mama doesn't eat gluten," Wren was saying.

"She does on weekends," countered Bella, "but Daddy may be vegan."

"Stace is vegan," Wren said.

"I thought Stace was a vegetarian, or pescatarian," Bella said.

"I think you're right," Wren agreed. "And Daddy may be just a *lil' bit* vegan,"

"Wait! What? Tad is a little bit vegan?" I asked, utterly confused. I was turning my head back and forth between the girls like I was watching a ping pong tournament.

And when they both looked at each other and laughed, I knew I'd been had, once again.

"You southern belles are playing me like a fiddle," I said, laughing.

"*Lil' bit*," Wren said.

166

44

We caught a little of the shoulder season,
Which is our second favorite.
-KERBY LODGE GUEST BOOK-

After the weather cleared, rays of sun pierced the freshly washed blue-gray sky. The waves and wind had ceased, and the sandy shores shone like scrubbed copper.

It was almost evening when Bella and Wren went with Hollis over to Gramps' cabin for dinner and canoeing with Jack and Stace. The girls all planned on pitching a tent and camping on the lakeshore. Jack had a new hammock he was dying to try out.

Along the way, they'd pick up Patti Lee Spondike. I knew the six of them would have a fun night at the Wildberry's safe harbor, and create the memories I wanted Bella and Wren to go home with.

The air was warm, but would cool off.

They would be wearing jeans with river sandals or hiking boots. Their all-weather fleece pullovers would be at the ready when the first cool breeze blew in, I knew. The loons would be gliding along the shore, which the kids would be able to hear because Gramps allowed no motors near his home. "I'm going to stay away from jet skis indefinitely," Bella had told us all.

A fire would be crackling, wafting delicious cherry wood tendrils into the dark blue starry sky—framed by the long needles of the fragrant white pine trees.

This was my Lake Michigan, the one I wanted the girls to fall in love with.

I *so* wanted to be with this group, on this night, but had to accept that I was their aunt, and not their friend, and not invited. As Luke said, theirs was not a world I fully belonged in.

Much like their parents, I could only fund it, monitor it, and long for it from a distance.

"It's just not fair," I commiserated to Alice after the girls drove off.

"Maybe your younger years were... incomplete," Alice said, eyeing me carefully. She must have heard about how my parents died when I was in my early 20s, and how I had accepted the responsibilities of Kerby Lodge at a young age.

"I hadn't thought of that, Alice," I said, truthfully.

"Soon enough, these kids will have to face adulthood head-on. But tonight, they have endless possibilities ahead," she said. "And we can too."

I nodded, thinking about what she was saying.

"It's a fine trick to appreciate what we have at any given moment, and not spend too much time looking in the rear-view-mirror," she said. "And on that note, I'm going to head home and convince a certain retiree to take me out for a perch sandwich and a movie."

After saying goodbye, I picked up my phone and dialed Luke, who was still at the school.

"What's up, Kaker Mayne?" he said, completely unaware of the effect that had on me.

"I've got some beautiful sea glass jewelry that's collecting dust, Luke Mayne," I said. "Should we take it out for a drive, or to Mitch's for dinner?"

"Yes to both," he said, "Pick you up in ten. I'll be the lucky man in the Jeep."

"Will you miss the apartment?" I teased as I picked at the back half of my cherry pie with the tines of my fork. I wasn't sure I could finish my desert after eating an entire serving of Mitch's baked mac and cheese, and a field green salad with pears, cranberries and goat cheese.

Mitch once again grabbed us from the back of the waiting line, and sat us at a premier spot by the window. I was beginning to wonder if he saved this table for the Kerby family.

"Won't your other guests fuss Mitch?" I had asked.

"Let them fuss," he said, "I own the joint." And flashing his famously bright smile, Mitch left us with a menu of the night's specials, and went to seat the next in line.

"I will not miss the apartment," Luke said, bringing me back from my wandering thoughts. "Although it's very cozy, and I always know where you are."

168

I laughed at that. "The girls have kept me on a short tether this summer, haven't they?"

Luke nodded.

"Having your nieces here has me wondering what life would be like if we had our own little family someday," Luke said.

"Oh?" I said, highly interested in this topic.

"I don't want to be an absentee father by going away to conferences," Luke told me.

I smiled at my husband.

"I appreciate the sentiment, Luke," I said, "but two weeks is hardly abandonment."

"And I don't think we should travel in July," Luke continued, not registering my comment, "not if it causes you so much stress as the owner of the lodge."

"Well that could be a problem," I said.

Luke raised his eyebrows at me and waited for me to continue.

"I've been looking at New Zealand—we should definitely go there next summer."

I told Luke that we had both lived such very different lives until we met. He was a man who never stayed in one place for very long. And except for my university years, I was the complete opposite—never straying far from the lodge.

"Somewhere in the middle, Luke Mayne, is our life," I told him. "And I think we should find it, together."

I saw him smiling at the corners of his mouth, and wanted more than anything to climb across the table and kiss that smile, I loved him so.

"You gave up so much for me when we got married, Luke," I said. "All I gave up was a few weeks of summer at Kerby Lodge—hardly anything, in the grand scheme."

Luke's piercing eyes were looking at mine as he almost imperceptibly shook his head.

"I gained the world, you crazy, beautiful nutcase," Luke said quietly, and smiled.

Before driving home in the open Jeep, Luke surprised me by turning onto a dirt road and making a slow trek to the shoreline. Few locals knew about this public access road, and hardly any tourists—it was an unspoken rule that we would not mention it to anyone we hadn't known for thirty years.

I made an exception for Luke.

"I'm grandfathering you in," I told him, "but don't abuse the privilege."

At the end of the tree line stands a gravel turnaround, and that's where Luke parked the Jeep. When he shut the motor and the lights off, we both instinctively leaned our heads back to look at the stars and the half-moon in the sky.

The water was trying to get our attention with its repetitive *sploosh, sploosh,* against the rocks and driftwood. We both flinched as a hoot owl flew from a branch behind us to another tree in front of us.

We mouthed "whoa," while turning to each other, not wanting to startle the owl.

The breeze was soft, and blew pine fragrances our way as it changed directions.

Gazing at the horizon, we could see the moonlight reflecting on the ripples and waves.

It was hard to take my eyes off the beautiful view, but when I turned to look at Luke, I saw that his head had been turned towards me, probably for a while. It sent a chill up my spine, in spite of the warm night.

I smiled, and leaned over to give him a lingering kiss.

"Did your sea glass jewelry have a nice time?" Luke said in a low voice, so as not to startle the owl, I supposed.

"It did," I whispered back, slipping my hand under his own and lacing my fingers through his, "but it wants to go home now."

45

The girls were back at Kerby Lodge the next day in a swirl of laughter and stories about their night on the shore—the moonlit canoe rides, the campfire, and the hobo breakfast they cooked in a cast iron skillet over the early morning embers.

Gramps brought them out a pot of hot percolator coffee, and a pan of cinnamon rolls he had baked in the oven to accompany their fireside sausages, eggs and fried potatoes. I could practically smell the sweet aromas of their breakfast as they spoke, and my stomach growled.

Bella and Wren talked over one another to Luke and I for a few minutes, telling us every little detail as we smiled and nodded. And then as quickly as they came into the lodge, they were on their way to the showers.

My heart swelled as I pictured the memories they made, and felt just a twinge of jealousy—but I wouldn't have traded my evening with Luke for a million moonlit canoe rides.

"Do you want me to pick up your brother," Luke asked me once they were gone, "or do you and the girls want to go to the airport this afternoon?"

"I thought I'd let Bella and Wren take the SUV themselves," I said, to a startled Luke.

171

Luke couldn't think of any words to say, so he just stared, stunned, until I spoke.

"They have a lot of catching up to do with their parents, and I'd just be in the way. Besides, it's only a twenty-minute drive. And Bella is very *cautious*." I said this to Luke, emphasizing the word *cautious*.

We both knew this was not always true.

She had not been nearly as cautious as we would have liked this summer at Kerby Lodge, but that was mainly regarding Max, and not her driving.

"You are very *selective* with your *memory*," Luke said to me with half a smile, mirroring my own inflections.

"But you are very *trusting* of my *judgment*," I said to him in return, smiling back.

"What is this weird conversation you two are having," Bella asked us both. She was standing in the great room with a towel over her arm, waiting for her turn in the shower.

After a moment of silence, Luke answered her. "We were practicing to teach English as a second language," he said. "But while you're here, Kay thinks you should drive the SUV to get your parents today, and I agree."

"We know you're a good driver," Luke continued, and went to get the keys.

Bella's mouth dropped open in surprise and delight.

"Just have pity on your poor old auntie and send me a text after you girls are safely at the luggage pickup, okay?" I asked. "And another when you have your folks in hand."

I knew that Tad would be surprised to see Bella and Wren at the airport without me, but these girls had been seriously shaken, and needed to find their footing again, and their confidence. They shouldn't be cowering from the world—they needed to conquer it.

They needed to go for a *thwim*, as Cody and Stuart Gray had taught us.

And if I was completely honest, maybe I was cowering from Tad, and delaying the anger he might feel towards me over my handling of the girls this summer.

"Kaker," Bella said a little tentatively, looking at me, "I couldn't take it if something happened to your new SUV."

"Nonsense Bella," I said. "Fender benders and scratches happen, and they can be fixed. I only want you girls to be safe."

Bella came over and gave Luke and I each a quick hug before heading towards the shower, shouting at Wren to step it up, because they had to go.

It was hours later when Tad and Selby returned with the girls, amid laughter and overlapping conversations. And multiple carry-out boxes from Mitch's restaurant, where they had stopped for dinner.

"Mitch sends his love, and pies," Tad said with a smile on his face.

After greeting everyone, we all sat on the burnt orange sofa as Bella and Wren gave Tad a photo album that they created with the old pictures.

Tad had tears in his eyes, looking first at the pictures of himself with me and with our mum and dad. There were photos of Tad sailing with Uncle Zeke, and repairing the old metal bikes in the carriage house. He shook his head in wonder.

"I really did love my years at Kerby Lodge," he said, "more than I knew."

Selby wiped away a small tear as she looked and laughed at the photos.

"Look at all that snow," she marveled in her southern drawl. She was looking at pictures of Tad outside with a shovel—standing up to his knees in white powder. This Atlanta girl saw a few dustings each winter, but had no idea what a Lake Michigan winter was really like.

That night, after Selby had gone to bed, Tad and I were left in the great room. I braced myself, but was surprised when he did finally speak.

"Kaker, I'm so sorry," he said.

Stunned, I listened as he apologized for throwing two teenaged girls at me for the summer, without any warning of what a handful they could be. Or how much they had protested coming to the lodge. "I can only imagine what they put you through," he continued.

Shaking my head, I wasn't sure how to respond.

"I had no idea how much I didn't know," I said, laughing softly.

I was relieved.

The girls had, of course, told Tad and Selby all about their adventures, and misadventures at Kerby Lodge. Tad went on to tell me how grateful he was that little Cody wasn't injured, and neither were the girls.

"Bella and I will take a run up to the hospital tomorrow, and check in on Max," Tad said. "Now that a few days have passed, I think we need some closure there."

I agreed, and gave Tad a hug before he turned towards the apartment.

As I was about to turn off the last light in the great room, Bella came wandering out.

"Have a minute?" she asked.

"Of course," I said.

After a few moments, Bella said, "I want to say I'm sorry for the way I've acted this summer. I was just rotten to you, and I made some bad choices."

I took a long look at this lovely young woman—on the cusp of making her own mark on the world. All the Christmas card photos flashed through my mind at once, just then, in sequential order. She was not a child, this dark-haired beauty.

So much like Fitz, and Tad.

"I have made bad choices, too, Bella," I said. "Raya loved you and Wren fiercely from the moment you were born," I said. "If she knew I'd kept my distance from you girls all these years, she would be fit to be tied. And rightly so."

She nodded.

"I'm sorry for all the lost time," I said, quietly.

Bella hugged me, and then she laughed softly to herself before sitting straight up.

"All right, Kaker," she said with a smile on her face, "let's have it."

"Let's have what?" I asked, truly stumped.

"You know, the Raya-isms. The wise Scottish sayings," she said. "I know you're dying to give me a *bit o' the brogue* before I leave…"

I was laughing at this point.

"…here's your one chance. As my penance, I will listen to you," Bella said.

I thought about that for a minute and then nodded. If there's one thing I have learned this summer, it's that when a teen says they're listening, you'd better have something to say.

"Okay, lass," I said, "but you're going to hear from both me *and* Raya!"

Bella pretended to groan, but I think she was secretly pleased.

"You're a Kerby, Bella," I said. "You're not perfect and never will be. But you're strong—like the full fetch of the wind. A mighty and sometimes dangerous power, until stopped. The trick is to stop yourself, instead of allowing other people to make decisions for you."

Bella took this in, I could tell.

"That's from me," I said, and Bella nodded solemnly.

"And as your grand mum would say if she were here," I continued in my Raya brogue, *"Ye are the most loved, highly esteemed grand-dahhter of Fitz and Raya Kerby, and dunna forget it wee lass."*

Bella laughed with delight, and smiled at me.

"I won't forget," she said.

46

Hi Kay, do you remember us? You were probably
Two years old when we saw you last, but we haven't changed a bit.
-KERBY LODGE GUEST BOOK-

"North meets South, meets vegan," I said to the good-natured but hungry crowd standing on the bluff between Kerby Lodge and Lake Michigan. "If you don't see what you're looking for, the Rusty Nail is right up the road."

"Amen," someone shouted from the crowd, as if I had said the meal's blessing.

As a light breeze moved the pine and the oak tree branches, and as last gasp swimmers and boaters enjoyed the clear waters and cloudless blue sky, I stood outside with my family and friends—laughing and eating.

My Labor Day cookout featured foods for everyone—the vegans, the vegetarians, the carnivores, and the farm-to-table crowd. Both of my new crockpots were being employed, along with several vintage pie plates, cake pans, and covered dishes.

Luke manned the grill, while a group of men stood around him, talking and laughing. There was Daniel, Tad, Patrick and Jack.

Uncle Zeke sat in an Adirondack chair, in a deep discussion with Hollis.

To my delight, Aunt June and Uncle Zeke had flown in for the long weekend. And I needn't have worried about where they would stay—they booked a guest room through VeRoom.com, with Hollis' help.

"It's a tax deduction," Zeke said.

Unbeknownst to me, Hollis had been working with Zeke and June all summer on profitability spreadsheets, so she would know when it did or did not make sense to book empty rooms to bargain hunters—and my aunt and uncle were delighted, I could tell, to be consulted.

Zeke wasn't ready to fully retire: "I see numbers in my sleep, Kaker."

Hollis had no idea how much she had changed Kerby Lodge for the better, but I did include a nice bonus with her last paycheck. "Profit sharing," I said. "Without your initiative, we would not have been booked solid all summer—and now, through the fall color season."

I told her that while I knew she'd have better opportunities than mine, I hoped she would consider coming back next summer. And I thanked her for suggesting that her mom, Alice, fill in for the busy autumn.

"She's such a *mom*, but she's pretty okay," Hollis said, dryly.

I noticed that Jack couldn't take his eyes off of the petite Hollis, even as he pretended to be part of the grill guard.

Alice was pretty okay.

Not only efficient, she might be one of the most welcoming presences Kerby Lodge has known since Raya herself held that distinction. Alice and her husband, Jim Fanning, I saw, sat at one of the picnic tables, laughing and talking with Nan and Sperry.

I gave June a quick hug as she brought out yet another casserole dish from the oven in the apartment, and insisted she fill a plate and sit down. She and Jennifer had been tirelessly helping me set out the abundant food table.

"I can manage the rest," I said, "and you two must be hungry."

A car pulled up in front of the lodge, and Beth Wildberry walked around to join the gathering. She was accompanied by both Gramps and Stace.

Daniel practically sprinted to Beth's side.

While Stace wandered off to join Selby, who was telling Bella and Wren more about their adventures in Vancouver, Daniel took the double-chocolate cake from Beth's hands and placed it on the food table. Then, taking Beth's hand in his own, he escorted both her and Gramps to where his parents sat to introduce them.

I felt nervous on Beth's behalf, though I needn't have been. I could see an outpouring of warmth all the way around, as several people scurried to find Gramps a comfortable chair, and get him a sampling of all the wonderful dishes.

Nan and Beth would have a million shared interests, I was sure. They both had a love for classic styles and rescued treasures. And a love for Daniel Mayne—the ultimate classic rescued treasure.

176

As for my brother-in-law, he was sharing the freshly remodeled A-Frame this weekend with Nan and Sperry, with mixed reviews. The elder Mayne's loved it, of course. But not so much Daniel.

"I feel like I'm back at my parents' house, now that their furniture is there," he said, uncomfortably. "I hate to say this Kaker, but I can't stay in the A-Frame after this weekend."

"I completely understand," I answered.

Imagine that. All the anxious thoughts I had about evicting Daniel from his on-again, off-again stays at the now luxurious A-Frame, and all it took was making it resemble his mother's house in Chicago.

Both Daniel and Luke Mayne adored their parents, I knew. But Nan had raised her sons to be strong, independent men—not ones who went "running back to mama," as Luke told me, when times were tough. I was starting to appreciate what a sacrifice that was for Nan, who longed for her sons, but rejoiced, I knew, in the successful, honorable lives they led.

As the sun set, we sat along the picnic tables chatting amiably. Many guests had coffee mugs in their hands, and dessert plates in front of them. Looking over, I was surprised to see Tad stand up, with a cold bottle of cream soda in hand.

Just like old times!

Clinking on the bottle with his fork tines, he captured everyone's complete attention.

"Here's to Kaker, and to the first annual Kerby Lodge Labor Day cookout," Tad said.

"To Kaker," everyone shouted.

Still standing, he stopped for a minute, and seemed to lose his train of thought. But then Selby reached up and took his hand, and he smiled at her. He had something to say, and she had given him the strength to continue, it appeared.

"Many years ago," he said, "I left Kerby Lodge and swore I'd never come back." He paused and closed his eyes for a moment or two. The crowd waited patiently.

"When I did return, it was to bury Mum and Dad, and then leave Kaker here all alone—something I've never been proud of."

I had no idea how Tad had felt, and my eyes burned as sudden tears filled them. Blinking hard, I tried to stay focused on my brother.

Luke reached over and put his warm arm around me.

"But with a busy life, and a growing family," he continued, "it was easy to forget my roots, and my heritage. And I might have continued, but," he said, "seeing my darling daughters nearly grown... seeing them get ready to leave my own home made me remember. My heart would break if they never came back."

He swallowed a lump in his throat, as did I.

Tad went on to tell us all, to light laughter, that Bella and Wren thought they were being punished by being sent to Kerby Lodge. But it was really to serve his own purposes.

"I wanted my daughters to connect with *my* past," he said, looking right at me, "only… I wasn't confident that I could make that connection. Not like Kaker could." Tad swallowed hard and finished his speech. Tears were rolling down many faces, I could see through my own tears.

"We can't go back and do things differently, as I sometimes would like to. But as long as there's a Kerby Lodge, this is where I plan to be every Labor Day weekend," he said, "and I hope you will be, too. In the meantime, let's raise a glass to something my mum Raya would say if she were here."

> *As the oak whose roots are strong, we will weather 'er life brings along.*
> *While moments come and then depart, love endures safe… in my heart.*

Tears stuck in Tad's throat.

After a minute, he was rescued by everyone shouting "here, here!"

Never before had I heard Theodore Kerby reflect any of Raya's sentiments, and it hit me that it was a void in my life he'd now filled—I'd often felt I was an only child, the way Tad had left home so quickly after high school, and stayed away until the death of our parents.

I stood up and went to meet my brother for a hug.

Tad's heart was coming home to Lake Michigan.

Hollis had been right. Families are messy. They are not perfect; not in our memories, and not in our photos. But they are beautiful in their own imperfect and messy way.

As I looked around at everybody, I couldn't help but think that the Kerby's were indeed coming back to Kerby Lodge. Only, I was no longer the teenager—Bella and Wren had taken that place. I had been bumped up a generation. So had Tad and Selby. Zeke and June had taken Gram's place, with Nan and Sperry close behind.

Daniel had his arm around Beth Wildberry, and Jack and Stace talked with Hollis.

Jennifer and Patrick were talking with Gramps, Alice and Jim.

It was a different family than any I could have assembled in my imagination, but a good group—and it would be the same, and yet different in subsequent years. I realized then that life moves and changes quickly. I reached over for Luke's hand and squeezed it tight.

And as the sun dipped a little lower, and the garden lights began twinkling in the trees surrounding the bonfire, I looked over at my good husband.

"Let's walk," I said.

47

Taking Luke's hand, we walked past the lodge guest wing, the swing sets, and the shuffleboard courts. Then past the chalets, and the larger cabins.

After walking up the steepest incline of the road, we passed the pond. The chatter of family was replaced by the wind weaving through the trees, and the gentle croaking of frogs.

"Where are you taking me, Kaker Mayne?" Luke asked softly.

"It's time to go home," I answered, with a smile.

As we reached the bend in the road, we looked down to see a single candle glowing at the bottom of a mason jar. It was sitting on a soft bed of pine needles, just inside the forest.

Luke stopped walking, and looked up at me, curiously.

When I said nothing, he gently pulled my hand and we walked a few more steps. Rounding the corner, there was another candle on the edge of the road—followed by another. And another.

A trail of lit candles shimmering in clear glass jars created a welcoming path for about twenty feet, guiding us to the deck of our home.

Luke gasped a little, as he saw that all the lights in the house were on. I gasped as well. Gazing up at the smile of wonderment on Luke's face, I knew what parents must feel like on Christmas morning, seeing something wonderful through the eyes of someone you loved.

We stepped onto the deck, and two new light-sensor lamps turned on next to the entrance. The lights were bright, but filtered through beautiful crackled crystal glass.

"Nice touch," Luke said, and stopped walking to look over at me.

"Should we go in?" I asked, and then added, "This is all new to me, too. I haven't been in the house since before you came home."

Luke smiled broadly at that. "Then let the big reveal begin."

We were stunned speechless with the renovation of Gram's house. Already ahead of its time with an open concept living room, dining space and kitchen, we could see nearly everything that had been remodeled as soon as we walked into the foyer.

The biggest transformation was the floor. Gone were the old shag carpets and worn tiles. In their place was beautiful and durable bamboo wood grain.

If that's all we'd done, it would almost be enough.

But then I looked to the left, and saw that Jack and Stace had carved out a coat closet near the entrance, with a bench, a tray for wet boots, and baskets for the numerous gloves and hats that are a winter necessity. Gram's antique Redware pottery vase now served as an umbrella stand. Luke and I nodded appreciatively.

Walking into the living room, Luke and I both laughed with joy as we sat on the newly upholstered Drexel sofa, and gazed at the chairs and tables. I couldn't believe it was the same furniture—every vintage piece had a fresh new life with bright fabrics.

The walls had been stripped of the metallic paper, and replaced with a neutral gray color, making the rooms look huge. The furniture was now the hero—and the artwork!

"Check it out, Kakes," Luke said excitedly, pointing to the largest wall in the room.

Jack and Stace created a photo gallery for us, featuring pictures of various textures and sizes. There was a large photo of Luke and I posing under a pine tree by the lake at our wedding reception—and another from our recent trip, hiking in the Alps.

Luke squeezed my hand as he pointed to the photo of my mum and dad at their wedding, and a family photo of the Mayne's, taken before the boys left home. There was an old grainy photo that we both had to take a closer look at. It was an enlargement of the picture the girls found in a box. The one of Tad, Luke and Daniel as young boys at Kerby Lodge.

Tears sprang to my eyes, and Luke put his arm around me. "Don't lose it now, Kay, we just got started," he laughed. I laughed too as I swiped my eyes with my shirt sleeve.

The basic footprint of the kitchen and dining room was the same, but reinvented through the eyes of our talented decorators. They replaced the old island top with a granite slab—one that hung over to create a breakfast bar, complete with vintage metal stools.

The Tulip chairs were still there, now paired with a more rustic and warmer table than the original round one. The total effect was eclectic and welcoming.

I could see in the newly painted kitchen cupboards that Stace had edited Gram's collection of serving pieces and cookware, and layered in a few of my new wedding gifts, along with some of my favorite pieces from the apartment kitchen.

Grinning so hard our faces hurt, Luke and I could see a small fire burning in the fireplace. We smiled up at each other, both thinking, I was sure, about our cozy winters ahead.

I leaned my head on Luke's shoulder.

"Let's go see the rest," Luke said, and I nodded and smiled.

We audibly gasped when we walked into our reconfigured master bedroom sanctuary. Jack and Stace had completely transformed this room by only leaving Gram's night stands, and by re-covering a sturdy vintage rocking chair with a modern chevron tapestry.

The bed itself was completely new.

It sat on the bamboo flooring with a plush rug anchoring a bench at the foot of the bed, and a drop-dead gorgeous Norwegian pine headboard at the other end. Downy soft pillows and comforters invited us to come in, and linger.

The sheets were turned down, I saw, with Swiss chocolates on the pillowcases. I did a double take when I touched the familiar sheets, and then saw a note sitting on the bed.

"The sheets you got for your wedding weren't the wrong size—the bed was!"

I smiled and showed the note to Luke.

"The next room is for you," I said to Luke, and leaned over to kiss him on the cheek.

"Wait," he said, grinning and caressing his pillow, "this room is for me."

"Come on," I said, smiling at him.

Opening the door to the second bedroom, Luke laughed out loud and hugged me before letting go of my hand to get a closer look. One entire wall was now filled with bookcases, flanking a sturdy teak desk in the middle of the room. In one corner, the leather Eames chair and ottoman sat with a wool throw, and a reading lamp.

"An office befitting the very scholarly Mr. Mayne," I said.

"You did this is for me?" Luke said, looking at me with so much love and amazement on his gorgeous face.

"I did," I said simply. "And check this out…" I took Luke to a wall hanging. It was a map of the world that I'd asked Stace to find. It had a pushpin in Lake Michigan, and a few more in the places we had just visited in Europe. "Let's see how many pins we can add."

Luke had a lump in his throat, I could tell.

"Don't lose it now, Luke," I said, through my own raspy voice. "We're not done."

The last bedroom door was closed.

"Storage?" Luke asked, and I shook my head.

I couldn't speak, and knew I shouldn't even try. I had no words to express what opening this last door would mean for the both of us. Taking a deep breath for courage, I simply turned the knob and stood with my husband in the doorway.

Together, we were speechless. I didn't realize I had been holding my breath until Luke reached both of his arms around me and pulled me into him so fully and so completely, that my breath expelled with an unexpected cry.

Putting his lips on my face, he kissed my tears and held me, as his own tears fell. Meanwhile, the little pine baby crib stood against the wall, on a soft yellow rug. Saying everything I couldn't.

Saying, "this is why my stomach has been so precarious this summer, and why I've been a little crazy."

Saying, "it wasn't the breakfasts in Europe, or the cookies in the lodge that made my waistline expand."

And saying that we could both do worse than becoming a bit more like Raya and Fitz, and a bit more like Nan and Sperry while we're at it. Because, *Och,* weren't they, and aren't they, the best and finest parents in all the world? And don't we hope to be so wise, and so loving, and just like them as we raise this sweet and most welcomed child?

A wee mid-winter Mayne.

48

And just like that, summer was over.
-KERBY LODGE GUEST BOOK-

The week after Labor Day

We will gather again for Thanksgiving at Tad's house, we all agreed. It would be the last time I'll be able to fly before the baby arrives. Zeke and June will join us, unless Zeke gets voted in as president of their gated community. In which case he would have to weigh and measure his responsibilities.

Zeke had been leveling an aggressive campaign against Walt Devot, the incumbent, he told us. But apparently, theirs was a beauty contest.

"The ladies love his hair," Zeke said, "but I've got the legs."

Before saying goodbye at the airport, Tad told me again how sorry he was for sending the girls the way he did, and blindsiding me. I told him I'd be returning the favor in 16 years.

When did the girls start calling me Kaker instead of Aunt Kay? I honestly couldn't say. The last days of our *Unforgettable Summer Vacation* were that much of a whirlwind. But I was sorry to see Bella and Wren leave—maybe more than they were.

The innkeeper's apartment was quickly clearing out—of both people and boxes.

By the time I finally took the unwanted wedding gifts for a drive, there were only a few things left. I had placed the *Dead Fish* sign above the angler's ice chest, the lava lamp in Luke's office of our Mid-Century Modern home, and put both crock pots in storage for next year's Labor Day weekend cookout. They had come in handy!

The lovely sheets, of course, were at home on our new bed.

And even the imported mosquito repellent candle had found a new home, in the garage. "It keeps the mice at bay," Alice told me, "without even being lit!"

Daniel came to load up his boxes from both the A-Frame and the apartment to transfer them to Beth Wildberry's business, where she had ample storage in her warehouse. Jack and Stace, along with Beth, came to help Daniel gather his things. The four of them seemed like a happy family as they laughed and joked and packed the modern Wildberry delivery van.

At one time, not so long ago, I had wondered if Daniel would continue to be the center of my world, as I had been the center of his—I was the girl and the lodge he needed to rescue, not realizing he was redeeming his own life and career in the process.

But as I watched him with Beth and the twins, I could see that there had been another family waiting in the wings who needed rescuing.

He would be, respectively, their hero, friend and great love.

The never frivolous Daniel would be strong and steady for Beth, weathering whatever insecurities she might have following her devastating divorce so long ago, until she realized that once the Mayne brothers were in your life, they were steadfast and true.

And as with the expensive mahogany pieces Beth salvaged, she would give Daniel a new life, and new purpose.

The twins would easily accept Daniel as their mother's paramour, because they had known him the longest. They'd watched his character unfold, and knew he would never toy with Beth's heart and life. He would blend in to the Wildberry family, without asking Beth to alter one iota of what she had built to safeguard her loved ones.

Daniel would offer Beth all of the security he possessed—his own trust fund would be at her disposal, no doubt. While insisting that her funds and accounts remain in her name only.

He would accompany Beth to restaurant openings and estate sales, as his schedule permitted, and come home, for the first time in his life, to true love and devotion. And to eyes that twinkled at his voice, and arms that threw themselves into his own.

Before they left, Jack and Stace took one last look around the innkeeper's apartment, and asked if we should consider tackling this space in the spring.

"Great income potential, Kay," Jack said.

Ouch!

For whatever reason, that comment felt like a blow, and I placed my hand protectively over my growing baby bump. For as much as I no longer wanted to live there, the apartment was the only home I'd ever known with my little family of Tad, Fitz and Raya.

It was the last Kerby remnant.

But then I remembered that Bella likened it to a museum, and she had been right. It was a museum to my past. I had a new home now, with Luke.

"Let's have a long winter's nap, and sleep on that," I said to the twins.

Before they left, Stace reminded me that she would see me in town in a few weeks, at Marj Maki's knitting class. While I always thought a sweater would be too ambitious, a baby blanket might be the perfect starter project. Plus, I had it on good authority that knitting was a great way to reduce stress.

Besides, knitting a wool blanket would keep me warm on cold winter nights, I told Luke. Of course, he had a few thoughts of his own on that.

But Luke did agree to watch the lodge office on Saturday mornings through early November, so that Alice could take the class, too. And after I convinced Jennifer to sign up, telling her that clumsiness loves company, Luke said that he and Patrick could put their heads together and work on their safety curriculum—when they weren't minding Carriage House Treasures, or making fresh coffee for lodge guests.

After politely declining a lift in the stuffed-to-the-rafters Wildberry truck, I made my way to the Mayne house, walking carefully up the Kerby Lodge road. Breathing in the sharp autumn air, and watching the first of the leaves tumbling off the branches, I wanted nothing more than to put my feet up on the sofa, and pull a wool blanket onto my lap.

A pot of chicken stew was simmering in the Dutch oven on the stove, I knew. And from the aroma of wood smoke in the air, I could tell that Luke had started a little fire to chase away the chill of the fall day.

We were down to the last two boxes from Gram's house that needed to be sorted. One, I knew, held all the photos that I'd kept with the intent of making an album or two this winter. I looked forward to setting up a table in front of our flat screen on snow days.

The other, I nearly tossed in the dumpster, sight unseen. So tired was I of ploughing through old dish towels with calendar years printed on them, newspapers with names and articles about people I never knew, and falling-apart church cookbooks.

186

"How many more tuna casserole recipes do I need?" I called to Luke, while he stood in the kitchen, making me a sandwich.

But at the bottom, under a stack of old tea towels, my hand fell on a book with a different feeling—unlike any other. This one had a thick spiral binding. When I pulled it into the light, my mouth fell open and I gasped so loudly that Luke came running.

"What is it Kaker?" he said, "is it the baby—are you all right?"

I nodded, but didn't trust myself to speak. All I could do was show Luke the book so he could read the cover for himself.

"*Journal*," he read out loud. "Is it..."

"Could it be?" I asked.

Opening it up, I could see that it was an innkeeper's journal—one of three that were at the bottom of a box I almost threw out like yesterday's news. My hands shook as I turned the first page, and saw Raya's unmistakable handwriting.

20 July 1972

Dunna know where the summer has gone, but it's half o'er already.

The wee bairn, the first babe Fitzwilliam and I haven't lost in early months, will be arriving shortly. A laddie, I'm thinking. If so, we will name him Theodore after Fitz's dearly departed Da. We are finally daring to hope, after so much loss. Two wee babes in the Heavenly Father's arms, but not in our own. And to think we will be raising him on the sunny and snowy banks of th' most beautiful water in the world: Lake Michigan.

Now then, a note about the Shaun Hennesy family. They've been coming the past two years, and don't they have sticky fingers – walking away with a few coffee cups on their way out the door each year.

They aught have a full set before long.

THE END

From the Author:

Thank you for reading *Water Dance*

I hope you enjoyed reading about this summer at Kerby Lodge as much as I enjoyed writing it. As I'm sure you know, reviews are the life blood of any author, so if you're inclined, I'd appreciate it if you could take a few minutes and leave a review.

Email me at kathy@kathyfawcett.com and visit kathyfawcett.com for updates, and to read my thoughts on writing and the writer's life.

Now available – official Kerby Lodge gear!

Now you can take home a souvenir of your time at Kerby Lodge, just like Kay's guests in *Water Dance*. Tee shirts, long sleeved tees, sweat shirts, hoodies and more. Check them out at kathyfawcett.com.

About Kathy Fawcett, author of *Water Dance*

Kathy Fawcett is an advertising writer and author of the Lake Michigan Lodge Stories, *Shoulder Season* and *Water Dance*. Her smart and funny characters are flawed optimists who think it's never too late to live an amazing life, in spite of life's bumps and challenges. Many of their own making! With stories set in the surf, sand, and snow of charming Lake Michigan towns, Kathy's readers will cheer for the true life underdogs, and laugh out loud at the observations and inner dialogue of her not-to-be underestimated heroines. Kathy has lived in Michigan most of her life, and has travelled extensively throughout the Great Lakes states. She met and married Steve Fawcett while at Northern Michigan University, and they now reside in western Michigan.